"Let me help you...

Simon implored her. "All [...] me."

He touched her gently, protectively, his fingers tracing the curve of her cheek. She couldn't move, couldn't speak. His thumb slid over her lower lip, sending a rush of desire straight through her.

Jolie looked into her dark savior's eyes. He really had rescued her tonight. He was beautiful...like an angel straight from heaven, except he was dark and alluring.

"None of this makes sense. It's crazy. Why would you risk your life for me?" she asked, filled with desperation and defeat.

He stared at her lips as she spoke, fighting the urge to press his own there, to comfort her and make her forget. "It doesn't matter why." He dragged his gaze upward to look directly into those jade pools of pure fear. "All you need to know is that I will."

Dear Harlequin Intrigue Reader,

We have a thrilling summer lineup for this month and throughout the season to make your beach reading positively sizzle!

To start things off with a big splash, you won't want to miss the next installment in bestselling author Rebecca York's popular 43 LIGHT STREET series. An overturned conviction gives a hardened hero a new name, a new face and the means, motive and opportunity to close in on the real killer. But will his quest for revenge prevent him from becoming *Intimate Strangers* with the woman who fuels his every fantasy?

Reader favorite Debra Webb will leave you on the edge of your seat with the continuation of her ongoing series COLBY AGENCY. In *Her Secret Alibi*, a lethally sexy undercover agent will stop at nothing in the name of justice, only to fall under the mesmerizing spell of his prime suspect!

The heat wave continues with Julie Miller's next tantalizing tale in THE TAYLOR CLAN. When the one woman whom a smoldering arson investigator can't stop wanting becomes the target of a stalker, will *Kansas City's Bravest* battle an inferno of danger—and desire—in the name of love? And in *Sarah's Secrets* by Lisa Childs, shocking secret agendas ignite perilous sparks between a skittish single mom and a cynical tracker!

If you're in the mood for breathtaking romantic suspense, you'll be riveted by our selections this month!

Enjoy!

Denise O'Sullivan
Senior Editor
Harlequin Intrigue

HER SECRET ALIBI
DEBRA WEBB

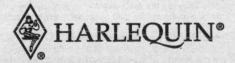

HARLEQUIN®

TORONTO • NEW YORK • LONDON
AMSTERDAM • PARIS • SYDNEY • HAMBURG
STOCKHOLM • ATHENS • TOKYO • MILAN • MADRID
PRAGUE • WARSAW • BUDAPEST • AUCKLAND

ISBN 0-373-22718-3

HER SECRET ALIBI

This edition published by arrangement with Harlequin Books S.A.

® and TM are trademarks of the publisher. Trademarks indicated with ® are registered in the United States Patent and Trademark Office, the Canadian Trade Marks Office and in other countries.

Visit us at www.eHarlequin.com

Printed in U.S.A.

ABOUT THE AUTHOR

Debra Webb was born in Scottsboro, Alabama, to parents who taught her that anything is possible if you want it badly enough. She began writing at age nine. Eventually she met and married the man of her dreams, and tried some other occupations, including selling vacuum cleaners and working in a factory, a day-care center, a hospital and a department store. When her husband joined the military, they moved to Berlin, Germany, and Debra became a secretary in the commanding general's office. By 1985 they were back in the States, and finally moved to Tennessee, to a small town where everyone knows everyone else. With the support of her husband and two beautiful daughters, Debra took up writing again, looking to mysteries and movies for inspiration. In 1998 her dream of writing for Harlequin came true. You can write to Debra with your comments at P.O. Box 64, Huntland, Tennessee 37345.

Books by Debra Webb

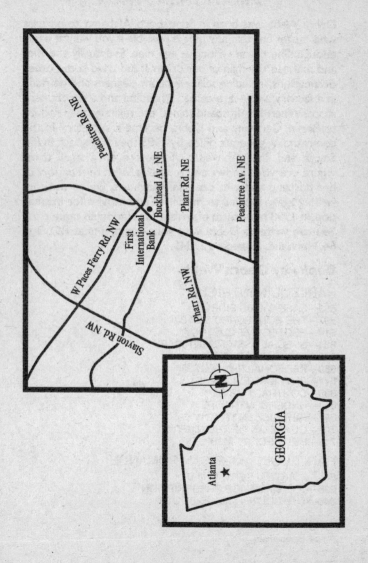

CAST OF CHARACTERS

Simon Ruhl—One of the Colby Agency's finest investigators. He will stop at nothing to bring down the man who murdered his former partner.

Jolie Randolph—Is she losing her mind? Falling victim to the illness that plagued her mother? As betrayal threatens her very life, who can she trust?

Mr. Knox—The bank's president and Jolie's boss. He is concerned that perhaps the stress of Jolie's new position is more than she'd bargained for.

Franklin Randolph—Jolie's father. He has a secret of his own. Will that secret destroy his daughter?

Mark Boyer—He has worked with Jolie for years. She received the promotion he wanted. How far will he go to prove they chose the wrong person for the job?

Erica Thornton—An advertising executive and Jolie's best friend. She wants to help…but can she before it's too late?

Renae Felder—Jolie's assistant. She has access to Jolie's calendar as well as her files. Is she as loyal as she'd like Jolie to think?

Special Agent Johnson—An old friend of Simon's in the FBI's Atlanta office. He is willing to help out a friend, but he can't look the other way when murder is involved.

Raymond "Big Ray" Brasco—The top mob boss in Atlanta. He doesn't take no for an answer.

Ray Brasco Jr.—The boss's son. He loves to play games, especially with the innocent.

Pierce "Max" Maxwell—Another agent from the Colby Agency. Max will provide backup and support for Simon. A former DEA agent, Max is always prepared.

This book is dedicated to a very special group of folks who have always been there whenever I needed them. I would like to thank the ladies and gentlemen, past and present, of Huntland Bank for their years of dedicated service and continued friendship. You have always added a special human touch to the business of banking.

Prologue

Victoria Colby stared out the window of her fourth floor office and tried not to think about the past. She'd had a difficult time pushing it aside lately. It wasn't like her to dwell on what she couldn't change. Unfortunately, it grew increasingly harder to do what she'd once been so very good at. Forgetting.

If she lived a thousand years she would never be able to forget the man she'd loved, James Colby. He had been her true soul mate. A man of honor...of courage. So few existed these days, it seemed. Her thoughts went immediately to Lucas Camp. Yes, there was another very much like her James had been. Lucas was the epitome of a good man.

A part of her longed to share the rest of her days on this earth with him, especially after coming so close to losing him only a few months ago. She shuddered as she thought of that island and those long hours when she hadn't known if Lucas was alive or dead. But something always made her hold back when it came to commitment, made her second-guess what her heart said. She did love Lucas, there was no denying that fact. Still, there was one thing that had prevented her from moving on with her life all these years.

James Colby, Jr. *Her son.*

She blinked, ruing the tears that never failed to surface when she thought of the little boy she'd borne. What good would her tears do? He was lost to her. If he were alive he would be a grown man now. She wondered if he would still look so much like his father. If he would be even half as honorable and courageous. If he were happy. If his life had been pleasant.

But most of all she wondered if he *was* alive. She'd waited all these years, hoping he was, and that he hadn't forgotten her or the happy home they had shared. Hoping that he would come back someday.

A heavy sigh escaped her lips. Most likely she would never know anything, and he wouldn't come back. But nothing would stop her from hoping.

"You wanted to see me, Victoria?"

The sound of Simon Ruhl's voice startled Victoria back to the here and now. She took a breath and composed herself before facing him. She had the agency. And she had her Colby agents—the very best in the business of private investigation. She had taken the agency her husband had started and gone all the way to the top. That was something. She did not have time to feel sorry for herself.

That realization galvanized her and she banished her troubling thoughts. They had a new case. One that was perfect for Simon Ruhl.

Victoria returned his smile and charged into work mode. "Please, have a seat, Simon. We have a new assignment to discuss."

When they had settled, she began. "Jason Hodges

is the head of the board of directors of Atlanta's First International Bank.'' She passed a folder to Simon for his perusal. ''As you'll see in there, he has a stellar record, as does his bank.''

She paused for a moment as Simon reviewed the contents of the file, then smiled when he looked up and asked, ''What's the problem?'' Nothing got past Simon. As a former member of the FBI, he'd had intensive training for just this sort of case. He would know that no matter how neat and tidy things looked on the surface, a great deal of trouble could lie just beneath. His Ivy League education and refined manner were perfect.

''Mr. Hodges has a great many important friends, including a contact or two in the Atlanta division of the Federal Bureau of Investigations. One of his contacts has given him a heads-up that his bank is on the list to be investigated for possible money laundering.''

His expression thoughtful, Simon commented, ''Raymond Brasco comes to mind.''

Victoria nodded. As she suspected, Simon had maintained his awareness of the top mob bosses affiliated with business in his former jurisdiction. When he'd worked for the Bureau, the Southeast had been a part of his territory. He was definitely the right man for this job.

''Mr. Hodges would like to determine if there is a problem, and if so, clear it up before it becomes a federal investigation. He has hired an outside auditing team. While the team evaluates the bank's accounting practices, you'll evaluate the employees. Being a member of this team will serve as your cover.''

Simon closed the folder and considered her words for a time. "Does Hodges suspect anyone?"

"Not really." Victoria shrugged. "At least he didn't admit to suspecting anyone in particular. He feels, however, that the most likely source for any such illegal activities would be in the international department, which is where he'd like you to start. The head of the department is a young woman named Jolie Randolph." Victoria nodded to the folder. "There's a photograph of her with some other employees at a Christmas party last year. Third from the left in the front row."

Simon pulled out the photograph and located the woman mentioned. "She's younger than I would have thought for a department head."

"In my opinion," Victoria offered, "her youth would certainly make her vulnerable. I believe…" Before she could stop it, the idea that if her son was alive he would be about that age zoomed into her mind. She blinked, then with effort pushed the thought away. "I believe she would be a good starting point."

Simon's dark, analyzing gaze collided with Victoria's. "I agree," he stated, as if he was fully focused on the conversation. But she felt his close scrutiny. He'd picked up on her distraction.

Annoyance flared, firming her resolve. She had to get her emotions under control. "Good."

"I'll get started right away," he added as he pushed himself to his feet. "Is there anything else you'd like to discuss?"

For a brief moment Victoria thought she noted a tightening in Simon's expression. Perhaps she'd misread the subtle shift. She resisted the urge to massage the ache that had started at her temples. This wasn't like her.

"That's all," she said quickly when she realized Simon was still waiting for her response.

After a succinct nod he left her office, closing the door behind him.

Victoria pounded her fist against her desk in frustration. She didn't have time for this. She had an agency to run. She didn't have time for the past.

The media had focused of late on several child abduction cases that hit entirely too close to home. That had to be the source of her problem. She had to find a way to keep her perspective. The past was gone; she couldn't change it.

And no force on earth could bring her son back.

Chapter One

Awareness came slowly. Jolie's head felt heavy and all fuzzy inside. Instinct warned that if she moved or opened her eyes pain would follow. But she had to wake up, had to move. She should be somewhere, doing something besides sleeping. If she could only wake up!

Gradually, her lids drifted open and she blinked rapidly against the brightness of the room. Focus came in unsteady stages until she could fully absorb her surroundings. The sun rising above the Atlanta skyline poured through the wall of windows facing her, spreading its light and warmth. Jolie frowned as her brain scrambled to place the images she saw. She was in bed. The sheets felt cool and smooth against her skin. What time was it? she wondered vaguely.

With her leaden body fighting her every inch of the way, she sat up, cleared her throat and pushed the hair from her eyes. Pain roared inside her skull. She moaned and held her head in her hands until the throbbing eased a bit. Another deeply entrenched instinct niggled at her, urging a response to some threat she couldn't yet comprehend. She licked her dry lips and grimaced. The taste in her mouth was oddly bitter. She needed a drink of water desperately.

With monumental effort she threw off the sheet covering her and dropped her feet to the lushly carpeted floor. Jolie immediately regretted the move. The room spun wildly for a couple of seconds. God, she had a hangover! She stilled. But she didn't remember getting drunk.

What day was it? She scowled and surveyed the enormous room and its lavish furnishings. From the elegant fringed and corded draperies drawn back to reveal the expansive windows, to the exquisite, dark wood furniture artfully placed about the room, the place reeked of wealth, but gave her no clue as to where in the world she was or how she had gotten there. Alarm trickled through her, but her fuzzy brain couldn't yet work up an appropriate reaction.

She stood on wobbly legs and groaned as she rubbed at the steady pounding behind her eyes. She shivered uncontrollably, then froze. Slowly, denial screaming in time with the throb inside her head, Jolie stared down at herself.

Naked.

Outright panic shot through her veins. She was naked. She surveyed the room again. Where was she?

Her chest constricted with fear as she spun around, desperately seeking anything—just one thing—that would provide some shred of evidence as to where she was.

Nothing.

The rich burgundy of the walls and carpet set off the dark mahogany of the heavy furnishings. The generous windows were all that saved the room from being unpleasantly dark. A pair of upholstered chairs occupied one corner like sentries at designated posts. Exquisite paintings graced the walls. But none of it looked familiar. This had to be a friend's place, Jolie reasoned with mushrooming dread. The alternative was unthinkable. She trembled at the conclusion forming in her lethargic mind.

Oh God. She swallowed convulsively. She wasn't at a friend's house. She didn't have time for many friends. She worked too many hours at the bank. Jolie had only one real friend, Erica, and this was definitely not her apartment.

Jolie's heart beat harder and faster, the blood thudding in her ears. The urge to flee was so strong now that her breath caught. Where *was* she? How did she get here? She felt confused and lost...

And frightened.

The sound of spraying water captured her attention, and bewildered, she turned toward the sound. An open door led to what appeared to be an en suite bathroom. Her feet had already taken her halfway across the room before the decision to move penetrated the dense cotton surrounding her brain. She stood stock-still in the doorway to the luxurious bathroom. An enticing, undeniably male fragrance scented the steamy air in the room. Stained glass window, huge sunken tub, gold fixtures and Italian tile all registered briefly, but it was the glass shower cubicle beyond all that to which Jolie's attention was drawn. Her eyes widened in confused disbelief. A man stood beneath the spray, steam rising above him like a billowing cloud. Dark hair, broad, broad shoulders, muscular back. She jerked back a step when her gaze traced the tight, well-formed buttocks and long muscular legs. She pivoted and took a couple of shaky steps, reality crashing down around her.

Jolie shook her head in denial. Her stomach roiled and the breath evaporated in her throat. She had never gone home with a stranger.

Never. Never. Never.

Clothes. She needed her clothes. Adrenaline burned a path through her veins. She had to find her clothes and get out of here. The man wouldn't stay in the shower forever. She needed to hurry!

Searching frantically, Jolie found her clothes scattered across a chaise longue, her shoes and purse on the floor nearby. She jerked on her panties and then the dress she had worn out to dinner last night: *Dinner*. Her hands stilled on the zipper at the small of her back. Flashes of memory slammed into her, making her dizzy again. Dinner with Erica at Carlisle's. Music. Laughing. People coming and going.

Jolie searched her memory, struggled to remember. What had happened after that? Why couldn't she remember leaving the restaurant? A new thought caused anxiety to twist in her stomach. Dinner with Erica had happened on Sunday night. That would make this Monday morning. She looked down at her left wrist and the gold watch she always wore. Eight-twenty. Her heart sank. She had forty minutes to get to work. And she didn't even know where she was or how she had gotten here…

Or with whom.

Silence snapped Jolie back to the present. The soft hiss of water had stopped. Fear such as she had never known before welled in her throat. She stepped into her shoes, grabbed her purse and, without looking back, ran from the bedroom.

SIMON WATCHED FROM behind the tinted windows of his SUV as Jolie Randolph hurried up the front steps leading to Atlanta's First International Bank. The short green skirt of her business suit showed off her exquisitely shaped legs a little too well for comfort. The fit of the matching jacket emphasized her slender figure. All that blond hair flowed around her shoulders like gleaming silk, making him want to thread his fingers through it. His groin reacted immediately at the thought. A muscle flexed in his tense jaw. Once Jolie disappeared through the towering ornate doors, Simon dragged his attention back to his cell phone.

"She just went inside." He listened to the annoyed voice of his client on the other end of the line. "No, it won't jeopardize anything," Simon argued impatiently, his foul mood steadily worsening. "Jolie is the weak link. I'm certain of that now." He tugged at the black tie around his neck. "I have an appointment with the bank's president at noon. I'll start applying the pressure right away."

He glanced up at the second floor of the four-story building, pinpointing Jolie Randolph's office. "Don't worry, I've got everything under control." Simon ended the call, then started the car's engine. He cast another assessing glance at the bank and his lips formed a grim line. If Jolie Randolph thought she had problems now, she should think again. Simon was relatively sure she was in deep. Though he still had a few doubts—doubts that bothered him—she was at the top of his suspect list. But she wasn't alone on that list.

A completely illogical anxiety needled him once more. He had to find a way to keep his objectivity on track here. He'd waited four long years for this opportunity. Whether Miss Randolph knew it or not, her nightmare had just begun.

"MISS RANDOLPH."

Jolie cringed inwardly as she paused in her hasty retreat from the conference room and this morning's status meeting. Despite her best efforts, she had been fifteen minutes late, and she hadn't missed the concerned looks Mr. Knox, the bank's president and her boss, had cast in her direction. She suppressed a weary sigh. There was nothing to do but pay the consequences. Producing her brightest smile, she turned and faced the older man.

"Yes, Mr. Knox?" She met his analyzing gaze head-on. "Was there something else you needed to speak with me about?"

Her boss drew in a decidedly long breath, crossed one arm over his chest and propped the elbow of the other on it so that he could stroke his chin. Jolie had the sudden, almost irresistible urge to tug at the collar of her blouse. She was still shaking inside from this morning's episode. Three cups of strong black coffee hadn't helped.

"Are you certain you're feeling all right, Miss Randolph?" His bushy gray brows furrowed in concern. "Your new position isn't proving more stressful than you anticipated?"

Jolie gritted her teeth behind her smile for about two seconds. She had received the long-anticipated promotion to vice president of investments just six months ago, and she loved it. Why did everyone, her own father included, have to be so worried about her ability to handle a little extra stress?

"Everything is fine, sir," she said calmly. "Just running a little behind this morning."

Mr. Knox tapped his cheek and studied her a moment longer. "You are the youngest vice president we've ever had here at First International," he reminded her. "And a woman," he added proudly. "Your well-being is of special interest to me, Miss Randolph."

Jolie's smile was genuine this time. She knew he meant well, however unnecessary his concern. "Thank you, sir."

Mr. Knox smiled knowingly. "You earned this promotion, young lady, and I have complete confidence in you. Like father, like daughter." With that, he turned and strode toward his own office at the far end of the hall.

Jolie released her pent-up breath when Mr. Knox was well out of hearing range. Only ten o'clock and the day had hit rock bottom already. With her own office just across the hall from the conference room, Jolie didn't have far to go to find refuge. She closed the door and crossed to her desk. In spite of all that had happened, she stole a moment to admire her spectacular view. The entire back wall of her office was one big window.

Just like the bedroom she had slept in last night.

Dread pooled in Jolie's stomach when she recalled the tense ride in the elevator to the first floor of the unfamiliar apartment building. Her heart had been pounding so hard by the time she'd reached the street and called a cab that she had been almost afraid she was going into cardiac arrest.

The entire episode was one big blur, and she barely remembered now what the building looked like. That was good, because she definitely wanted to forget the entire event. Oddly, she had found her car parked outside her own apartment building, though she specifically remembered driving it to dinner the night before to meet Erica. Had she gone home afterward? Then gone out again? Why couldn't she remember? With no time to consider the puzzle further, Jolie had rushed into her apartment, showered and changed, then hurried to work. And still she was late for the weekly status meeting. She'd bet her father had never been late, not once. He'd retired as president of the bank almost six years ago, and he'd left large shoes for all others to fill—including Jolie.

Put all of it out of your mind, she ordered. Forcing away the frightening memories as well as the self-deprecating thoughts, Jolie tossed her datafax onto her desk, put away her purse and buzzed Renae, her assistant, to pass along her requirements for the morning. Jolie dropped into her high-back leather chair and closed her eyes for just a minute. To her dismay, in that brief moment of total relaxation, this morning's few vivid mental pictures played through her weary mind. All images of the man. She shuddered at the thought that a stranger had touched her. She swallowed hard. How could she have allowed that to happen? She had been at dinner and...

Erica. She could call her friend. Erica would know what happened. But when her recorded voice came across the line, Jolie remembered that her friend had left early that morning for a business trip. She wouldn't be back in Atlanta until late tomorrow afternoon.

Heaving another disgusted sigh, Julie settled the receiver back into its cradle. The vision of the man—

naked, with water streaming over his sculpted body—ricocheted through her still somewhat groggy mind. She shivered. How could she have gone home with that man—been with him—and not remember it?

Fear gripped her, cutting off her breath, at the answer that echoed in her brain. She shook her head as if to deny the thought. She was not like her mother. *No.* That was not possible. She would never be like her. Her mother had been very ill. The last two years of her life had been a roller-coaster ride through the final stages of severe mental illness. Jolie swallowed hard. Living with her mother had been like living with two different people those last months. One had been the loving woman Jolie had known all her life, the other someone she barely recognized. But her mother had been too weak to fight the demons that had haunted her for far too many years to count. Jolie was strong. She was fine.

"Fine," Jolie repeated out loud.

Renae rapped lightly on the door. Jolie sat up straighter and composed herself. She would not think about any of that right now. She had a job to do. A job she loved.

She motioned for Renae to come in, then squared her shoulders and forced her attention to her work.

"Miss Randolph…" Renae stepped into the office, a folder clutched to her chest. "We have a slight problem."

Jolie frowned, then brightened. Good. Work problems she could handle. "What's up?" she asked, as her assistant moved around her desk to open the folder and spread the papers out before her.

"There's a fifty thousand dollar discrepancy in this account," Renae said tentatively.

Jolie scanned the number and then the name of the account holder. This was one of *her* accounts. "There must be a mistake," she murmured promptly.

"I felt certain you would be able to take care of it," Renae suggested hesitantly.

Jolie resisted the urge to frown at her assistant. Of course she would take care of it. Why was Renae behaving so nervously? Realization hit Jolie like a mallet between the eyes. The audit. Next month's annual audit had everyone at the bank jumping through hoops.

"It's all right, Renae," Jolie assured her. "I'll handle it. I'm sure it's nothing more than an input error."

Renae smiled weakly. "You're right. I don't know why I was so worried." She shrugged. "This audit thing has us all out of sorts."

"It'll be over soon."

"Oh, I almost forgot." Renae looked thoughtful. "A man called for you this morning before you arrived, but he wouldn't leave a message."

Panic pricked Jolie. "Did he leave a name?"

Renae shook her head. "He just wanted to know if you made it to work all right."

Panic stabbed deeper. "He hasn't called again?"

"No." Renae frowned. "It was all very odd." She smiled wickedly then. "But he had a voice that would make a nun want to break her vows."

Jolie tamped down the anxiety climbing into her throat. She refused to consider that the call could have been from the man in whose bed she had awakened. She intended to put that episode out of her head. She would simply pretend it hadn't happened. It was the only way to maintain her sanity.

But how could she pretend last night hadn't happened? Jolie's stomach knotted. There could be serious consequences. Dear God, what had she done?

"I'll get to the bottom of this right away." Jolie tapped the folder and attempted a confident smile.

"Let me know if you need anything else," Renae said as she skirted the desk and headed for the door.

"Thanks," Jolie replied vacantly. She watched through the glass wall that separated her office from the hall as Renae hurried away. She and Jolie had worked together for years. Renae was tall, slender and very attractive. She bragged about having a new boyfriend every week. Renae had always considered Jolie too uptight and straitlaced for her own good. What would dear old Renae think if she knew the man who had called this morning was probably the stranger Jolie had slept with last night?

She shook off the troubling thoughts and dived headfirst into her work.

BY NOON JOLIE KNEW she had a serious problem on her hands. She had exhausted every possibility, to no avail. The money had simply disappeared. She chewed her lower lip and allowed the one word that no banker ever wanted to consider to slip into conscious thought.

Embezzlement.

But how could that be? This was her account. Though Jolie could have turned over all her accounts to the other department head in foreign investments, she had kept several to oversee personally. These were special clients who preferred Jolie's brand of financial strategizing. Mark, now the sole head of foreign investments, was not happy about it. He had all but accused Jolie of keeping the best clients to herself.

But Jolie was the boss now, and Mark had known better than to push the issue. Besides, she didn't take him for a guy who really went to the mat on an issue. He'd always seemed a little spineless to her. However, Mark was good at his job. Not once had a client complained about his work. He was dependable and charming, and enormously diplomatic with the bank's clients. And smart, Jolie had to admit.

She stared at the computer printouts before her. She had to be missing something. The money could not have disappeared into thin air. And she sure as hell hadn't taken it. An uneasy feeling accompanied that thought, but she pushed it away. She did not take the money. And she never made mistakes like this.

Jolie flattened her palms on her desk and stood. Enough. She needed a break. She would go out, have a nice quiet lunch and recharge her batteries. The episode this morning still had her shaken, and she hadn't eaten all day. Lunch was just what she needed. Jolie grabbed her purse and headed for the door. There was a nice restaurant only a couple of blocks away. The place would be crowded at this hour, but knowing Jolie's discomfort with crowds, Lebron, the owner, would find her a quiet table in the back.

She paused before taking the stairs down to the first floor, placing her hand on the ornate banister and surveying the crowded lobby. First International's was the largest and most elegant gallery in Atlanta. Accustomed to seeing it every day, Jolie sometimes forgot just how lovely it really was, with its marble floors, intricately carved wood decor and leaded glass windows. She smiled. She loved this bank. Patrons lined up before the tellers' windows, others hovered around tables, filling out deposit and withdrawal slips.

Atlanta's financially elite trusted this bank. Trusted Jolie.

She noticed Mr. Knox doing what he did best—mingling with the customers and promoting bank-client relations. He suddenly moved to one side, and the man with whom he was speaking came into full view. Jolie's next breath caught in her throat. He was tall and breathtakingly handsome, with hair as dark as midnight worn in a short style that complimented his angular features. That bronzed complexion completed the heart-stopping picture.

She couldn't recall ever having seen a man quite so handsome. His black suit fitted so well it had to have been tailored just for him. She frowned. Why simply staring at a good-looking man should make her heart flutter like a hummingbird's wings she couldn't fathom. She gave her head a little shake and silently scolded herself for behaving so foolishly.

At precisely that moment the man's eyes met hers. Time suddenly stood still. The customers, the sounds around them faded into insignificance. There was only Jolie and this stranger looking at her so intently, as if he knew her and they shared some secret. As if…he wanted her. Jolie had the oddest feeling that they had met before. She tried to think of where or when, but couldn't perform the necessary cognitive function. She could only stare into those dark eyes. A restless sensation started deep in her belly and spread outward, making her too warm beneath the silk of her two-piece suit.

"Jolie, there's an urgent overseas call for you."

She whirled abruptly, almost relieved at the summons. Renae's expression was as anxious as her own must certainly be flustered. Jolie's cheeks burned with embarrassment when it dawned on her that she had blatantly stared at the man, would still be doing so if Renae hadn't interrupted. She closed her eyes to banish the image that continued to linger there. She just couldn't concentrate today.

"Hurry, Jolie, he says it's imperative that he speak to you." Renae thrust out a note.

"I'm coming," she muttered, taking the piece of paper and starting toward her office. She had every intention of going straight there, but hesitated, glancing one last time at the place in the lobby where the stranger had stood.

He was gone. She dismissed the peculiar feeling of connection and hurried back to her office.

Taking a second to catch her breath, she inhaled deeply, then slowly exhaled. Once more and she was ready. Boy, she was a real mess this morning.

"Good afternoon, Mr.—" Jolie glanced at the note Renae had shoved into her hand "—Millard, this is Jolie Randolph. How may I help you?" She frowned at the words *First Royal Cayman Bank* scribbled beneath the caller's name.

"Miss Randolph," the man began in a thick, distinguished accent. "I was most concerned when I received your latest deposit transfer without the usual instructions."

Deposit transfer? Jolie wrinkled her forehead in a frown. At a Cayman bank? That was impossible. "I'm sorry, Mr. Millard, are you referring to an account belonging to a client of this bank?" She considered crossly that it might be something new Mark was involved in. It would be just like him to leave her in the dark.

"No, no, *mademoiselle,* I'm referring to your *personal* account."

Jolie almost laughed out loud. "My personal account? I'm sorry, there must be some mistake."

"Mistake? There is no mistake. You make a transfer twice per month, and always with precise instructions as to your wishes." He cleared his throat impatiently. "Now, may I have your instructions?"

Ice formed in Jolie's stomach. This was wrong. It had to be a mistake. She didn't have a foreign account. She never made personal transfers of an international nature—with or without instructions. Her heart slammed mercilessly against her rib cage.

"Miss Randolph?"

Jolie shook her head in denial of the question she was about to ask. But she had to know. "Would you give me a balance on the account, please, Mr. Millard?"

Jolie slumped back in her leather chair when he recited a number just shy of one and a half million dollars. The room shifted around her, and for one long moment Jolie thought she would faint. This was insane. It had to be some ridiculous mistake.

"You've made six deposit transfers since setting up the account in person just three months ago," he added, obviously miffed that she had no recall of the transactions.

She couldn't deal with this now. It couldn't be happening. She had never been to the Cayman Islands, much less set up an account at their most prestigious bank. She had to end this call. She had to think. Jolie drew in a harsh, steadying breath and interrupted the man's continued protests that he had her signature on file, and other personal data. "Mr. Millard," she said stiffly, "I apologize for the misunderstanding. Please handle my latest transfer as you did the previous one." She had no idea what that meant, but it seemed to appease the man. "Refresh my memory, if you would, regarding my other deposits."

Ten minutes later, Jolie dropped the receiver back into its cradle. She felt numb. This was crazy. She couldn't have taken a trip, set up a foreign bank account and transferred more than a million dollars into it without remembering....

Could she?

A memory surfaced with gut-wrenching swiftness. Of her mother swearing to her father that she hadn't bought the clothes and jewelry he'd found hidden in her closet. She'd sworn she hadn't made the unexplainable charges to credit cards amounting to thousands of dollars. Someone else had done it. Why wouldn't anyone believe her?

Jolie wet her lips and shook her head. No. That wasn't happening to her. She wasn't like her mother. She closed her eyes to hold back the tears. She had loved her mother so, but she wasn't like her. Jolie wasn't ill. She was fine. Just fine.

She swiped the moisture from her eyes and took a deep, bolstering breath. She surveyed her office, taking solace in the numerous plaques and other accolades that adorned the two side walls. She was not her mother. This was some sort of mistake and Jolie would straighten it out. Then she would put this entire deplorable day behind her.

Lunch would just have to wait.

ONE POINT FOUR MILLION dollars. The amount deposited in the Cayman bank was exactly the amount

missing from the client accounts Jolie personally
maintained. Each discrepancy, date of withdrawal and
amount matched a deposit transfer to the First Royal
Cayman Bank.

Long after the bank had closed Jolie sat staring at
the figures. She pressed her fingertips to her throbbing
temples and closed her eyes. There was no explanation for it. The money was simply gone.

Oh God.

Another wave of near hysteria washed over her.
The audit. She had to undo this damage before anyone
noticed. She winced. Renae had already found one
discrepancy. What if she discovered the rest before
Jolie could fix everything? She would never be able
to smile at her assistant and assure her that it was a
simple input error.

Okay, she told herself, squashing the panic exploding inside her. She could take care of this. It was late
now. She needed a clear head and a fresh start to undo
this sort of damage. First thing tomorrow morning,
Jolie would redeposit all the money back into her clients' accounts. She would close the Cayman account
and pretend it had never happened.

But it did happen, a little voice mocked.

She pushed herself out of her chair and grabbed
her purse. She had to get out of here. Maybe she
could reach Erica at her hotel in St. Louis. Jolie
needed a plan. Instead of feeling sorry for herself, she
would work the problem out. This time next month,
when the audit was over, this whole nightmare would
be just a bad memory.

She hesitated at the door as a vague image flashed
in her mind's eye—the fleeting impression of a man.
She stood very still for a time and attempted to re-

capture the fragment of memory, but couldn't. God, she was tired.

She turned off her light and locked the door behind her. Everyone else had gone home already. A quiet dinner was just what she needed. But she didn't really want to go home right now. Her place would be too empty, allowing too many questions to haunt her.

The night watchman let Jolie out the side entrance, the one closest to her car. In her haste this morning, she hadn't bothered parking it in the garage. She'd never been to Lebron's for anything other than lunch, but it was handy and familiar, so she decided to head there now. She glanced up at the September night sky and its winking stars, and forced herself to relax. Tomorrow would be better.

It couldn't possibly get any worse.

Chapter Two

Jolie strolled the two blocks to Lebron's Restaurant. Neon lights flickered and flashed, competing with the streetlamps and passing car lights. She felt better already just being away from her office. Later, when she got home, she would call her dad, just to hear his voice. Everything was going to be okay.

She was okay.

There had to be an explanation for all that had happened.

Lebron's night manager showed Jolie to a table in the back, where it was quiet. She thanked him and ordered a glass of white wine from the waiter standing by. In an effort to quell the compulsion to fidget, she folded her hands in her lap and waited patiently for her drink.

She was fine, she assured that little voice that lingered in the back of her mind. The whole thing could be straightened out. Mistakes happened. This had to be a mistake. There simply was no other explanation.

Jolie shifted to a more comfortable position, then stretched her neck from side to side. Despite her efforts to relax a prickly sensation rushed over her skin. She knew the signs. Panic was bearing down on her.

She inhaled a long, deep breath and then exhaled slowly. She was okay, she told herself again. She'd had panic attacks before…occasionally. All she had to do was focus on relaxing and she could stop it before it went any further.

In the beginning, her mother had taken medication for anxiety and panic attacks. Eventually even that hadn't helped. Jolie shook her head. This wasn't the same. She didn't need medication. She wasn't like her mother.

The memory of waking up in a strange man's bed broadsided her, and she jerked helplessly. The strange call at the office Renae had mentioned, the numerous accounts with discrepancies… The trip she didn't remember taking—hadn't taken! The personal account at a Cayman Bank she couldn't possibly have opened—all of it whirled inside her head. Jolie closed her eyes and resisted the urge to scream or cry or both. How could this be happening? She had worked so hard. She was just beginning to see the fruits of her labor. The promotion, the professional recognition—she was on her way. She was the youngest VP ever. All of which she had accomplished on her own, after her father had retired. Why did this have to happen now? Tears stung behind her closed lids.

The waiter arrived. Jolie snapped her eyes open and managed a strained thank-you as he set her wine before her. She reached for the delicate stemmed glass, but her hand shook so badly that she dropped it back onto her lap beneath the table. She blinked back the tears. She would not cry. She would not fall apart. She was stronger than that…stronger than her mother. She would fix this somehow.

"A beautiful lady should never dine alone."

Jolie's head shot up. Her gaze connected instantly with the dark, mesmerizing eyes of the man she had seen in the bank's lobby earlier that day. For one second she wondered if her mind had somehow conjured him up. No…he was real and somehow familiar. Heat flowed through her, vanquishing the ice-cold dread and panic threatening to choke her.

"May I join you?" he asked in a deep, velvety voice that touched some chord deep inside her.

Who was this man? she wondered briefly, before she found her voice to answer. Why had he been in the bank today? What had he and Mr. Knox been discussing? And why was he here now? The other tangle of troubles flitted through her mind all over again, as well. Missing money…missing hours. Had last night's disaster started with her talking to some stranger?

Probably.

Jolie firmed her resolve and stared defiantly at the sinfully handsome man. "I hate to injure your pride, sir, but *if* we've met before it proved unmemorable." Damn it, she fumed. Did she look that easy? She never had before.

A slow smile slid across those firm, full lips, making the man even more handsome, if that was possible, but only adding to her growing frustration. If she had ever seen that smile before she would indeed remember it.

"I'm sorry," he murmured. "My name is Simon." He held out his hand. "And you are?"

Jolie looked from those mesmerizing eyes to his hand and back. His charm proved far too potent to resist. She placed her hand, however hesitantly, in his. Long, tapered fingers closed around hers, and just like

earlier today, something passed between them. Heat
and something more. Something she couldn't quite
define.

"Jolie Randolph," she heard herself say.

"It's a pleasure to make your acquaintance, Jolie
Randolph." Before she knew what he intended, he
bent slightly and lifted her fingers to his lips. The kiss
was nothing more than the faintest brush of his
mouth, but the effect was devastating.

He smiled again, this time at her startled expression. It was as if he fully realized the effect he had
on her. "As I said, you're much too beautiful to be
sitting here all alone."

Jolie tugged her fingers free of his. Her skin was
on fire where his lips had touched her. This was ridiculous. He was a stranger. The image of the man
in the shower this morning flitted through her mind's
eye. The last thing she needed was another stranger
in her life! "You should choose another pickup line,
Mr...."

"Ruhl," he told her, his gaze never leaving hers.
"Simon Ruhl. And you haven't answered my question, Miss Randolph."

Jolie sipped her wine, taking a much-needed break
from his intense gaze and pretending to consider his
offer. Why was she encouraging him? Flirting, that's
what she was doing. She should simply ignore him
so he would leave. "Actually, Mr. Ruhl, I only want
a quiet dinner alone." She allowed her gaze to meet
his once more. Lord knew she already had enough
trouble. And this man had trouble written all over his
amazing face.

His eyes were too knowing and offered a most

tempting escape. "You look like a lady who could use someone to talk to, *Jolie.*"

The way he said her name, the way the French intended, made her tremble. What was it about this man? "Mr. Ruhl—"

"Simon," he insisted.

She focused on the pale amber liquid in her glass for a time. "I'm afraid I wouldn't be very good company."

Simon sat down across from her. "Why don't you let me be the judge of that," he said quietly, soothingly.

She should have been incensed that he took such liberty, but instead she looked into those dark eyes and for one moment wanted to believe that this man, this stranger, cared. What the hell? she decided. She had nothing better to do. The thought of going to prison for embezzlement, or worse, skittered through her mind. But not tonight, she decided suddenly. Definitely not tonight. She'd had enough stress for one day. Time to relax and just be. She needed to forget for a little while. Just for tonight.

Tonight she intended to put her troubles out of her head. She was going to chat with Simon. She had every intention of finding out who he was and what business he'd had in her bank today. She smiled at her companion. Why not? It certainly sounded better than sitting here beating herself up for what she couldn't explain. His answering smile sent her heart into overdrive, immediately short-circuiting whatever her next thought should have been.

Simon gestured to the waiter and ordered a glass of wine for himself, and another for her. "So." He turned that intense focus fully on her then. "What would make such a pretty lady look so sad?"

Boy, he didn't beat around the bush. Sad, huh? Jolie supposed it would be impossible to conceal the life-altering events of her day. But she wasn't about to tell him her personal business. Besides, she was supposed to be getting her mind off that subject.

"Bad day at the office," she hedged as she fingered the stem of her glass. "Speaking of which…" her gaze moved back to his "…do you come to my bank often?"

"I never mix business with pleasure," he answered, doing a little hedging of his own. Then he closed his hand around hers, effectively stilling her restless fingers and completely derailing her thoughts. "And I'm a good listener, Jolie."

The words startled her for a moment, but the desperation twisting inside her made her weak. She wanted to believe the sincerity in those beautiful brown eyes more than she had ever wanted to believe anything in her entire life. What did that make her?

Reckless? Maybe. Definitely desperate.

"Tell me, Simon," she said suddenly, not taking the time to analyze what she was going to say, "Do you think we become our parents?" Regret and fear rocketed inside her. She had loved her mother; how could she want to banish her memory? But she did. Jolie wanted to pretend it all away. To act as if it had never happened.

Something resembling concern flickered in his penetrating gaze. "No," he said emphatically.

"No?" Jolie studied his handsome face for some hint of what he might be thinking. It was as if he knew what she wanted to hear, but how could he?

"Absolutely not," he said resolutely. "We're all unique. There's no one else in the whole world like you, Jolie." He tasted his wine. "No one," he added softly. His thumb caressed her hand in a most distracting manner.

She stiffened her spine against the delightful shivers he inspired, and drew her hand away. "You don't believe in the sins of the father—or mother—and all that jazz?"

He shook his head slowly. "We choose our own path. Nothing is preordained."

Jolie lifted her glass to her lips, her hand feeling suddenly cold without his warm touch. She drank deeply, then smiled at the man watching her so very intently.

"I hope you're right, Simon." She licked her bottom lip, then chewed it thoughtfully for a second or two. "I really hope you're right."

"Tell me about you," he insisted, the words laced with silky charm. "Why don't you tell me everything about Jolie Randolph?"

Now there was a lethal question. He couldn't possibly know that he'd just tossed out the one query she felt suddenly unable to answer. Who was she? Had she really taken a trip she didn't remember? Stolen money from her own bank? The panic reared its ugly head once more. She swallowed tightly, then forced down a gulp of wine. She prayed he didn't notice the way her hand shook.

"I'm afraid you'd be rather bored with the subject," she answered. She hated that her voice sounded so thin...so nervous. Where was the strength she knew herself capable of? Where was the real Jolie?

Maybe she was losing more than merely her grip on reality. Maybe she was losing herself.

LATER SIMON INSISTED on walking Jolie to her car. The stars twinkled even brighter now, and the crescent moon looked like a lopsided grin high in the dark Atlanta sky. She smiled, feeling much, much better. Maybe it was the company. She stole a glance at the man beside her.

In profile, Simon Ruhl looked dark and mysterious and utterly gorgeous. Jolie felt giddy with excitement—something she hadn't felt in a very long time. He was charming and intelligent. Every touch, every look made her feel warm and tingly inside. It was foolish, she knew. But she couldn't help herself. She felt like a college coed again, out on a date with the most popular hunk on campus.

"This one's mine," she said as they neared her Lexus. She stopped when she reached her door, and turned to her dark savior. He really had saved her tonight. Just then his right hand came up to brush a tendril of hair from her cheek, and her breath stalled in her lungs. He was beautiful. Perfect, she amended, like an angel straight from heaven, except he was dark and alluring in a sinful kind of way.

She shivered. The wine, she told herself. It had to be the wine making her so giddy, though she'd consumed scarcely more than a glass. She hadn't reacted to a man like this since... Who was she kidding? To her knowledge, she had never behaved so irrationally.

"Thank you, Simon," she said softly, "for dinner and for taking my mind off...things." She looked up into those dark, dark eyes and forgot anything else she would have said.

''Thank you, Jolie Randolph,'' he said just as softly. ''For a truly memorable evening.'' His smile turned teasing, his words reminding her of her earlier comment about any previous meeting between them having been unmemorable.

Blushing at the faux pas, Jolie stared at her hands as she unconsciously wrung them. How could she have said something so totally lame to this charming and completely gorgeous guy?

As she looked up again Simon moved closer, effectively trapping her between his body and the car. Instead of the warmth he had inspired all evening, unease stole over Jolie. The realization that it was dark and she was alone with a man she had met only hours ago hit her hard. This morning's panic gripped her all over again. What was wrong with her? Why hadn't she seen this moment coming? Fresh panic slid down her spine and she flattened herself against the cool metal surface of the car. She had behaved this irrationally before. *Last night.*

Simon's gaze latched on to hers, and she knew the instant he recognized her fear.

He stepped back. ''I apologize,'' he murmured. ''It wasn't my intent to crowd you.''

''I…I should go.'' Her heart racing, she reached into her purse for her keys. Her relief was almost palpable when she found them on the first try. She nearly dropped the jangling ring, and Simon took them before she did just that, unlocked and opened her car door.

''Good night, Simon,'' she said, as politely as she could manage when he held the keys out for her. She turned away, hoping he wouldn't notice her jerky movements. She wasn't losing her mind; she had already lost it. Simon probably thought she was…

She didn't even want to think about that. This was why she'd never had a decent relationship. She couldn't trust herself, so how could she trust anyone else? It seemed ludicrous that she'd only this moment realized that sad fact.

"Wait," he murmured.

Jolie froze. Slowly she faced him once more, the car door between them like a shield. "Yes?" She tensed when he reached toward her, but something in his eyes kept her from drawing away.

He touched her gently, protectively, his fingers tracing the curve of her cheek. She couldn't move, couldn't speak. She could only stare into those intense pools of darkest brown. His thumb slid over her lower lip, sending a rush of desire straight through her. She trembled. As she watched, he slowly, so very slowly, lowered his face to hers. Jolie's heart thumped hard. She should run, she knew, but she simply could not. He bypassed her lips and kissed her cheek, lingered there a moment longer than necessary.

"Be safe, Jolie," he whispered against her skin.

Before she could respond, he turned and walked away.

And she still knew nothing at all about Simon Ruhl.

SIMON SAT IN THE concealing darkness of his SUV and watched as Jolie hurried up the walk leading to her apartment building. A few minutes later the lights came on in her living room, then the bedroom. The blinds closed and Simon shifted his gaze to the street in front of him. She was safe at home…

This time.

He closed his eyes, tightened his grip on the steering wheel and fought the urge to go up and stand guard at her door. Clenching his jaw, he tried without success to banish the images that haunted him. The way she smiled, so innocent and trusting. Her blond hair falling around her shoulders, feathery wisps caressing her face. And those eyes—wide, luminous green with tiny flecks of gold. She looked so fragile and sweetly feminine.

He wanted to keep her safe. That wasn't part of his job. He would not let anything get in his way this time. Brasco was going down one way or another.

Simon opened his eyes and stared up at the now dark windows. He had to remember that Jolie Randolph was a suspect. No matter how he reacted to her physically, and despite his instincts to the contrary, he had to remember that Jolie was most likely up to her pretty neck in serious trouble. Laundering money for the mob was no petty crime. And if she was involved with Brasco, she deserved whatever she got. Simon shook his head at the degree of stupidity he had shown tonight. He had bent his own first rule by kissing the woman. Brief though it might have been, a kiss was a kiss. It wouldn't have been a big deal if he hadn't been affected, if he hadn't wanted to pull her into his arms and make it real…but he had.

Still wanted to. Simon swallowed back the need welling inside him. He swore hotly at his inability to maintain control. He could deal with the fact that Jolie Randolph was beautiful. He could even deal with the slender curves of her toned body. But what he couldn't turn away from was the sweetness, the innocence she radiated. She needed protecting, and the damned woman didn't even know it. Whether she was guilty or not, which she probably was, Jolie was on the edge of a deadly precipice. Men like Raymond Brasco played for keeps. Big Ray or any one of his men wouldn't hesitate to kill someone like Jolie if she got in his way or failed to live up to his expectations. Simon knew that firsthand. The input he'd received from his old colleague at the local Bureau office backed up his every conclusion.

Raymond Brasco hadn't changed.

Jolie Randolph was in over her head.

And Simon wanted to protect her more than he wanted to take his next breath, and that didn't sit well with him. He had a job to do. This time it was personal. He had been watching Jolie and another of the bank's employees, Mark Boyer, for two weeks now. He likely knew more about them than they knew about themselves, particularly Jolie. Simon's former life in the Federal Bureau of Investigation had taught him every trick in the book when it came to profiling a suspect.

Unfortunately, the time he had spent watching Jolie had somehow evolved into something deeper for him. And that was dangerous, for her and for him. Not to mention it had never happened to him before. Not once. But her circumstances were different. There were things she apparently didn't know. Things that could tear her whole world apart.

Tomorrow his cover at the bank would be put in place, facilitating the investigation requested by the bank's board of directors. By hiring the Colby Agency to look into the situation, they hoped to head off a full-fledged federal investigation and possible scandal in the media. With major corporations making the headlines every day, the board wanted action fast.

Monitoring Jolie's and Mark Boyer's activities at work would be much easier from the inside. The contact he'd had with Jolie so far would keep her off balance. Simon needed her unsure of herself. Boyer was slick, and tripping him up wouldn't be easy. But Jolie was vulnerable. Simon had no choice but to work this investigation from the most accessible angle. He had to turn up the heat and intensify the pressure until she snapped. Time was of the essence. The feds wouldn't be put off much longer. They wanted answers.

The memory of the way Jolie had looked at him in the bank today when she'd hesitated at the top of the stairs, as if she had remembered something or recognized him, seeped into his thoughts. Simon's response was immediate and savage. That connection had been real, at least on some level. He had felt it too strongly to believe otherwise. And tonight, there had been something...some sort of mental as well as physical connection.

If he couldn't maintain his objectivity where Jolie was concerned, Simon would have to reconsider his strategy. Maybe even turn over her after-hours surveillance to another investigator at the Colby Agency. Simon had already taken a risk by not telling Victoria that this case hit far too close to home, was personal to him on more than one level. She wouldn't like it if she discovered his omission. He would simply have to deal with her disappointment and irritation when the time came. All that mattered to him at the moment was bringing down Brasco. If Simon had to call in backup to prevent getting in too deep with Jolie, then he would. That would keep him on track and out of trouble.

But he had a feeling that no force on earth could keep him from wanting Jolie.

Chapter Three

By early afternoon on Tuesday Jolie breathed her first real sigh of relief. She had corrected each account discrepancy, and then carefully covered the original erroneous transaction with a side note alluding to an investment maneuver. Though she hated the dirty way it made her feel, at least no one would ever have to know that the money had been missing. Jolie refused to consider that her actions were much like those of someone in denial.

Just like her mother.

Not today, she told herself firmly. Today she wasn't going to think about that.

Jolie shuffled through her messages, prioritizing them as she went. Most of her regular work had gone by the wayside this morning. Now she would spend the afternoon playing catch-up. Simon's handsome face suddenly filled her mind's eye. Heat flared inside her at the memory of his gentle touch. He had listened with such complete understanding as she'd rambled on and on about how screwed up life could get sometimes. Though she hadn't actually told him anything that had happened, she'd talked all around it, and he'd listened. She had felt so much better by the end of the night that Jolie was certain Mr. Ruhl must be a psychologist or counselor of some sort. She'd completely forgotten to pursue the issue of why he'd been at her bank talking to the president. She supposed he was just another customer.

She smiled. A very nice customer.

And definitely the best looking man she had ever seen. Remembering the sweet way he had kissed her cheek sent a shimmer of desire through her. Now that kiss was one for the record books. He had given of himself and his time all evening, and expected nothing in return. Just a simple peck on the cheek. Heat swirled beneath Jolie's belly button. Well, perhaps that wasn't quite an accurate description of Simon's brief kiss. There had been a definite fire kindling between them, but he had held back because she was uncertain, and she felt truly grateful. If Simon had taken advantage of her, she would have fallen apart. *Vulnerable* was apparently her new watchword.

She still hadn't been able to reach Erica to ask about the missing hours Sunday night. Jolie forced away the knot of emotions that accompanied the memory of waking up in a strange bed. She would not think about that until she could question Erica and more accurately analyze what had taken place that evening. Besides, she rationalized, she'd had her hands full this morning with straightening out her accounts. There was nothing she could do about her strange behavior Sunday night. It was done. She just had to make sure it never happened again. The fact that she had dined with another stranger last night, had even allowed him to walk her to her car, disturbed her, but not nearly as much as it should.

Why did her life feel suddenly so out of control?

"Knock, knock, madam vice president."

Jolie looked up to find Mark Boyer loitering in her doorway. She could have done without a visit from him today. But he was here, and to tell him to jump out the nearest window, as she would have liked to do, would be rude and unprofessional.

"Good afternoon, Mark," Jolie said in her most chipper tone. "What can I do for you today?"

Mark plopped into a chair facing Jolie's desk. "Actually, I wanted to do something for you," he suggested in that patronizing voice that made her want to cringe.

Jolie folded her arms over her chest and leaned back in her chair. This should be interesting, she decided. "And what would that be?" Mark Boyer never did anything unless it would somehow prove to be to his own personal benefit.

He pulled a concerned face. "I'm worried about you, Jolie," he said with what appeared to be complete sincerity. She knew better. "You don't look well. I think you need a break. Take a few days off. I'll cover for you."

Anger flared so fast that she barely kept herself from lashing out at him. *Calm, Jolie,* she chastised herself. *This is business. You can't go biting off the heads of co-workers. Mr. Knox wouldn't like it.*

"Thank you for your concern, Mark," she said evenly, then smiled weakly. "But I'm fine."

He splayed his hands. "Don't try to fool me, Jolie. I've known you too long. You're not fine." He shook his head and made a negative sound in the back of his throat. "Not by a long shot." He smiled suddenly, as if some realization had dawned. "Why don't you take a little vacation?" His tawny brows formed a perfect V above his calculating eyes. "Didn't you spend a couple of days in the Caymans two or three months ago?"

Jolie's heart almost stopped. A chill sank clear through to her bones. She blinked rapidly to mask the fear in her eyes. "I said I'm fine, Mark," she repeated firmly. "I don't need a vacation."

He looked taken aback. "Well, you don't have to get testy about it, Jolie. It was merely a suggestion."

She stared at him coolly. "I'll take your suggestion under advisement. Now—" she turned to the reports scattered on her desk "—if you don't mind, I have work to do." She glanced up once more. "And I'm expecting a client," she added by way of dismissal.

He stood, then shrugged. "Don't say I didn't warn you," he remarked casually. "Burnout happens all the time in high-pressure positions. Just ask your father."

Seething at his comment, Jolie didn't bother to respond, but shot a cross look in his direction. Her father hadn't burned out, he'd simply chosen to retire early. Even a decade after her mother's death they had both struggled with the memory and heartache. How could Mark throw that painful past in her face?

It was hard to believe that she had once considered him a nice guy. They had worked together for two years. Together they had made quite a name for themselves in the investment department. The "golden ones," that's what they had been called. She and Mark had made a great team. Both were young, with him only a couple of years older than herself, and equally ambitious. Both had blond hair; she supposed that was where the golden part came in. And though she and Mark had never been friends in the true sense of the word, they had maintained a good working relationship.

But Jolie's promotion had changed all that. Everyone had expected him to get it instead. He was a man, after all, and he did have a few months seniority on her.

But she had gotten the promotion.

And he hadn't forgiven her yet. Had even made remarks behind her back that it was only because her father had once been president and the board had respected his reputation.

When Jolie's anger receded all that was left was panic. He had said she'd taken a trip to the Caymans. That couldn't be. She hadn't gone anywhere this year. Fear crept into her racing heart. But why would he say it if it weren't true? What did he have to gain by lying? It wasn't as if she couldn't verify whether she had taken a trip or not.

She just didn't remember taking one.

Her mother had disappeared for days at a time that last year of her life. She would return with no memory of where she had been or what she had done. Jolie's lower lip trembled with the emotion swelling inside her. And then, finally, when her mother could bear it no longer, she had ended her misery.

That wouldn't happen to Jolie. There had to be another explanation.

"Jolie, I'm glad you're in," Mr. Knox announced from her door.

Jolie snapped to attention, automatically standing to greet the bank's president. She manufactured a smile. "Good afternoon, sir." She racked her brain to recall if they had an appointment. Surely Renae would have reminded her. Jolie felt weak with worry.

Maybe Renae had reminded her and she had forgotten the meeting, anyway.

"I hope we're not interrupting anything that can't wait," Mr. Knox said as he gestured for someone to enter ahead of him.

Jolie waited expectantly for the mystery guest to step around Mr. Knox and into her office, but when he did she wasn't prepared.

Simon Ruhl.

"Hello, Miss Randolph," he said in that low, velvety voice as he approached her desk and thrust one square hand in her direction.

Confusion reigned supreme. Jolie stood there, stunned, for one long, awkward moment.

"Miss Randolph, this is Simon Ruhl," Mr. Knox explained. "The bank has contracted his firm to conduct an informal audit just to make sure we're ready for the real thing next month."

"Hello," she managed to murmur. She placed her hand in his, and those long fingers curled around hers, sending heat straight to her center. He held on a beat longer than was proper. Jolie could feel the strength radiating from him, a strength obviously tempered in his gentle touch. Those dark eyes held her in a sort of sensual trance. She shoved the foolish reaction aside.

"Simon has assured me that we won't even know he's here." Mr. Knox chuckled. "That may be a bit optimistic, but I'm sure he'll manage without getting in anyone's way."

Simon's reassuring smile was pure charm. "Trust me, Mr. Knox, First International's board of directors would never have hired me had they not had complete faith in my ability to conduct this audit with little or no disruption in the bank's status quo."

Mr. Knox crossed his arms over his chest and rocked back on his heels. "Of course," he agreed. "I certainly want to facilitate your effort to that end, so I've decided to have Miss Randolph be the liaison between you and the bank's staff."

Jolie felt the color drain from her face. She couldn't do this. This man knew too much about her already. Though she had revealed nothing earth-shattering, she had allowed herself to be far too open with him. He read her too easily. He made her feel things she shouldn't feel. How could they start over with that kiss between them?

Jolie turned to Mr. Knox, praying that she could change his mind. "To be honest, Mr. Knox, I believe Mark would be a much better liaison," she said, as calmly as possible with her heart racing for some unseen finish line.

Mr. Knox seemed to consider her suggestion for a moment. Jolie didn't dare look at Simon. If she looked, she would only get trapped in that rich coffee-colored gaze again.

The bank president tapped his cheek thoughtfully. "Mark would be a wise choice, as well," he said noncommittally. He looked from Jolie to Simon.

"Actually," Simon said, drawing Jolie's reluctant attention back to him, "I've heard so much about Miss Randolph's stellar reputation, I was really hoping to have a chance to work with her." Something remotely akin to amusement flickered in his challenging gaze.

"The board is very proud of Miss Randolph," Mr.

Knox interjected quickly. "But you'll find her a tad shy of the limelight."

Simon's smile was triumphant. "I'm sure we'll work quite well together."

Mr. Knox clapped him on the back. "Excellent. Well…" he turned to Jolie "…I'll leave Simon in your capable hands, Miss Randolph."

Jolie nodded, unable to marshal a verbal response. She waited until Mr. Knox had closed her door behind him before she turned back to Simon.

"Why didn't you tell me?" she demanded, irritation overriding all else at the moment.

In a blatant act of intimidation, Simon allowed his gaze to roam down her body, then slowly back up to her face. Her fists clenched at her sides. Every nerve ending stood at attention—whether from anger or awareness, Jolie couldn't quite determine. Simon slid his hands into the pockets of his trousers and studied her until he had satisfied whatever motivated his arrogant behavior. This was a side she hadn't seen last night. Maybe this man wasn't all she'd thought he was.

"The décision wasn't made until this morning," he said quietly. "There was no reason to tell you last night. Last night," he added, "was pleasure. *This* is business."

"You should have told me anyway," she said in a scathing tone, as upset with herself as she was with him. "You knew who I was. You took advantage of the situation."

With slow, deliberate steps, Simon walked around her desk to stand directly in front of her. Too close. Her breath caught when he leaned even closer, but for the life of her she couldn't move away.

"No," he murmured, so near to her that she felt his warm breath on her lips. "I didn't take advantage of the situation." He looked at her lips as if he might just kiss her right then, right there. "I could have." His gaze connected with hers once more, heat and challenge smoldering there. And something else—a knowing that made her nervous...restless. "But I didn't."

Jolie stumbled back, stopped by her desk. "My assistant will...will show you around," she stammered. Unable, or maybe unwilling, to take her eyes off him, she fumbled across her desk until she found the right button and pressed it. "She'll introduce you to the rest of the staff."

"Yes, ma'am." Renae's voice resonated from the intercom.

If her life had depended upon it, Jolie couldn't have said what exactly it was at that moment that held her speechless. Something about the way Simon looked at her made her want to eagerly submit to his wishes. But she couldn't...wouldn't. Her survival, personal as well as professional, depended on it. The silence stretched on, screaming between them for endless seconds.

"All right," he finally said, the words somehow releasing her from that surreal hold.

"Renae, would you step down to my office, please," Jolie instructed in a breathless tone that made her want to kick something.

Simon's gaze held hers captive a moment longer before he turned and walked back around to the front of her desk to wait for her assistant. Relieved to have some space between them, Jolie attempted to focus on the matter at hand.

"How long will you be with us, Mr. Ruhl?" she asked with as much authority as she could dredge up.

He shrugged one broad shoulder. "That depends on you, *Jolie.*"

She shivered. He did that on purpose—said her name that way. "Mr. Ruhl—"

"Simon," he insisted.

"I don't think—"

"I do," he challenged.

Where had that obstinate attitude been last night? Better yet, where was the charming, soft-spoken gentleman she'd met? She resisted the urge to squirm beneath the intensity of his continued gaze, and, to her credit, managed not to look away. Fortunately, Renae walked in just then and shattered the building tension.

"Renae—" Jolie cleared her throat "—this is Simon Ruhl."

"Renae Martin." She offered her hand. "It's a pleasure to meet you, Simon."

Jolie frowned. Renae had never once called her by her first name. When Simon took Renae's hand, the woman all but melted into a puddle. Jolie rolled her eyes. Was no one immune to the man's charm when he chose to turn it on?

"Renae," Jolie said, drawing her assistant's reluctant attention. "*Mr. Ruhl* is conducting a preliminary review in preparation for next month's audit. I'd like you to introduce him to the department heads and see that he has whatever he needs to complete his work."

Renae's smile was wide and appreciative. "I'll be happy to." She turned to Simon. "Follow me, sir."

Simon took one last, lingering look at Jolie, and this time she did squirm. He gave her a final curt nod, then walked out the door. Jolie had the distinct impression that she had just been warned.

SIMON RECEIVED THE GRAND tour of Atlanta's First International Bank, not that he needed it. He had studied the blueprints already. He knew the place as well as the engineers who had designed and built it. The introductions hadn't been necessary, either, but he had gone through the motions. He had conducted a thorough background investigation on every employee at the bank. Though Jolie and Boyer were his prime suspects, Simon left nothing to chance. The Bureau had trained him well in that regard. The Colby Agency expected nothing less.

He glanced at his watch. Two o'clock. Boyer was in a meeting with clients. Jolie had seemed pretty nervous an hour ago. Time to rattle her cage again, he decided. Simon strode down the long, carpeted corridor. All the offices, with the exception of the bank president's, had glass walls facing the hall. He supposed that architectural design fostered an air of trust. Everything was out in the open. Even the conference room provided a full view from the hall as well as the lobby. The rear wall in each vice president's office was solid glass as well, providing a noteworthy panorama of the Atlanta skyline, but leaving only the partitions between each office to provide any privacy.

Simon paused at Jolie's open door. He thought about knocking, but decided against it. With her back to him, the telephone tucked between her ear and shoulder, she appeared deeply engrossed in her conversation. Simon walked slowly, soundlessly to her desk.

"No, no, that can't be right," she argued with the

person on the other end of the line. Jolie sighed in obvious frustration. "Yes, I know that's what it says. Okay, do you have the hard copy of the receipt?" There was a pause. "I'd like to see it. No, I'm not disputing the payment. I…I was considering going back and couldn't remember the hotel I stayed in before."

She was lying. He didn't have to see her face; he could hear it in her voice. Subtle inflections that the average person wouldn't notice gave her away.

"No, not for bank business…no." Another long pause. "A copy will be fine," she said with clear relief. "Yes, thank you." Jolie turned around and hung up the phone. Worry was etched across the delicate features of her face. Simon's gut clenched automatically at the pain he saw there. If he could only get her to come clean with him. It would save him a lot of trouble and quite possibly save her life. His presence finally penetrated her preoccupied state. Her head came up, surprise, then fear registering.

"Planning on taking a trip?" he asked pointedly, pressing her with the precise look he knew undid her composure. Her discomfort was immediate. The satisfaction Simon usually garnered when he knew he had hit his mark was not forthcoming. Yet he remained standing, adding to her mounting distress. He needed her off balance. He told himself repeatedly that last night's performance had been necessary…but a part of him knew that it had been all too real. It wouldn't happen again. Maintaining his perspective was far too important to risk any sort of slip.

She licked those full, pouty lips. "I…" She shook her head as if to clear it. "I was checking on a hotel for a friend." She glanced at her desk, then back up at him. "Was there something you needed?" She frowned. "Renae will—"

"You," he interrupted smoothly. "I would like to review your computer files now."

Jolie shot to her feet so fast her chair banged against her credenza. "I haven't had lunch yet. Could we do that around three?" She was gathering her purse before Simon had a chance to answer.

She was putting him off. He inventoried her posture once more. Putting him off, hell, she was ready to run. Time to move in for the kill, so to speak.

Simon shoved his hands into his pockets and shrugged. "Sure. I missed lunch, too. We can discuss your work history over lunch."

Her hopes of ditching him dissolved like a sand castle in the evening tide. "We can do that," she offered hesitantly. "As long as you don't mind stopping by my place," she added quickly, her eyes brightening with renewed inspiration. "I have to pick up a quarterly report I left at home."

Simon smiled. She hoped—no, she prayed, he would bet—that her ruse would deter him. Jolie Randolph was not nearly good enough at playing this game. The stakes were far too high for him to give even one inch. "I'll drive," Simon offered, to her utter dismay.

A THOUSAND QUESTIONS flitted through Jolie's dazed mind on the ride from the bank to her apartment. She had taken a trip to the Caymans. She closed her eyes and drew in a shaky breath. The proof was in her travel folder. She blinked furiously to stem the tears brimming. Oh, God, how was this possible? She had left on Friday morning and returned Monday afternoon. Her own files showed the time away from the office, and the signature on the travel voucher was hers. At least it looked like hers.

Oh God!

Nausea rose in Jolie's throat. She fought to contain the emotions churning inside her. She felt more than certain that Simon would not appreciate her soiling the interior of his fancy sport utility vehicle. She swallowed, then breathed deeply and slowly. Calm, she had to stay calm. The travel clerk had acted as if it took an Act of Congress to pull Jolie's three-month-old travel record. She needed to see the actual hotel receipt with her signature. She had apparently failed to keep a copy for the file in her office. The travel office wouldn't provide her with a copy of the receipt until tomorrow.

And she had to know today.

Jolie had also spent twenty minutes on the telephone getting the details on the one purchase that appeared on her personal credit card during that lost weekend. According to their records, she had evidently purchased a T-shirt in a George Town tourist shop. If that were true, the garment had to be in her apartment somewhere. Jolie stole a glance at Simon. How could she do that with him dogging her every step? She plowed the fingers of one hand through her hair and tried to hang on to her vanishing composure. It wouldn't do for her to come unglued in Simon's presence. He knew too much already. And Jolie had the feeling that he suspected her of some wrongdoing, as well. Why else would he be watching her so closely? Trying to shake her up? She closed her eyes. God, what had she done?

"Here we are," he announced as he parked the car.

Jolie looked from Simon to her building and back. It wasn't until that moment that she realized she hadn't given him directions or her address.

"How did you know where I live?" she demanded, trepidation taking all the sternness from her tone.

He gifted her with a little smile that altered only one side of his mouth, yet affected her entire being. "I know where everyone who works at the bank lives."

"Why?" Her voice sounded strained.

"Because it's my job," he told her bluntly, as if that answer should not only be clear to her, but reasonable as well.

Stunned, she watched him get out of the car, walk around the hood and open her door. Who was this man? A suffocating panic tightened her chest. Did she really want to know? Maybe she should just go back to the office and do this later.

No. She had to know now. She couldn't live a minute longer than necessary with the uncertainty.

The trip to the fourth floor was made without a word spoken and with only the echo of their footfalls in the building's blandly painted stairwell to break the deafening silence. Forcing a calm she didn't feel, Jolie unlocked the door to her apartment and pushed it open wide as she hurried inside. "Make yourself at home, Mr. Ruhl, I'll only be a minute."

"Nice place," he remarked nonchalantly.

Jolie didn't look back. She didn't have to. Simon Ruhl's tone might sound casual, but there was absolutely nothing casual about him. She knew that now. He was no doubt already thoroughly appraising the way she lived for inclusion in his report to the board of directors. Her decorating was very contemporary and Spartan, but her purchases were fine quality. Would he take one look at her choice in furnishings and decide she lived above her means? Did they suspect her already?

Did they know about the money?

By the time Jolie reached her bedroom, she was practically running. Drawing a deep breath, she took a moment to collect herself. Five minutes. That's all it would take for her to check the closet and the drawers. Simon wouldn't know what she was up to. He would be too busy analyzing her lifestyle, weighing it against her annual salary. She rushed to the walk-in closet and riffled through the contents. She checked her entire hanging wardrobe twice.

Nothing.

She moved back to the center of the room and took stock. It had to be here somewhere. If she had given it to Erica, her friend would have worn it at least once. Her father would certainly have done the same. Jolie had never seen any such shirt. That meant it had to be hidden somewhere.

She checked her watch and swore. Six minutes had passed. She had to hurry. Her hysteria rising with each passing second, she jerked first one, then another drawer open. She inspected the contents as quickly as possible, tossing to the floor whatever got in her way. Lingerie, hose, sweaters, socks. No T-shirt sporting a Cayman Islands logo.

Damn it, she had to find it. Jolie tunneled her fingers through her hair and surveyed the mess she had made. Her eyes latched on to the night table near the bed and its two unopened drawers. She rushed to the bed and dropped to her knees. The top drawer held magazines, tissues and aspirin. Frustrated now, she jerked the bottom drawer a bit harder than necessary. It pulled all the way out and overturned, its contents spilling across the beige carpet.

This was useless, she ruminated as she stuffed two scarves and a Georgia Bulldogs cap back into the drawer. She paused when she reached for the last item on the floor—a neatly folded white T-shirt. Everything inside her stilled, and she didn't even breathe. Almost in slow motion she reached out and picked up the cotton garment. She shook out the folds, and something fluttered to the floor, but Jolie couldn't take her eyes off the screen-printed blue sky and matching blue waters, the sandy beach and brilliant disc of golden sun.

She shook her head in defeat. This couldn't be. There had to be some mistake. The T-shirt fell to the floor as her now limp hands dropped into her lap. What was she going to do? Something white on the carpet drew her splintered attention. It was an elegantly embossed business card. Frowning, she picked it up and read the printed words. ''J. L. Millard, First Royal Cayman Bank.'' A telephone number was listed beneath the name.

Panic snaked around Jolie's neck and tightened. She had stolen her clients' money. She had taken a trip, purchased touristy stuff…spent the night with a stranger. And she had no memory of any of it.

''There's a call for you from the bank.''

Jolie jerked around. Simon loomed in her bedroom doorway. There was no way he could miss the fact that she had trashed the room in an obvious search for something.

She placed the business card on her night table and scrambled to her feet. ''A call?'' she echoed with rising hysteria. "I didn't hear the phone." Jolie ran her damp palms over her jacket, pretending to straighten it, then glanced at the cordless extension on the table by the bed. Had she turned off the ringer and forgotten?

Simon simply stared at her in that intent, unnerving way of his. "It's Renae," he said carefully.

"I'll get it in the living room," she suggested as calmly as her churning emotions would allow. Summoning her courage, Jolie took a step in his direction. She had to get out of here, away from him.

"Did you find your report?"

Jolie clenched and unclenched her fists. Her fingers were numb. She felt lightheaded. "No," she said tightly as she forced one foot in front of the other until she had crossed the room. She paused at the door, waiting for him to step aside.

One second turned to five before he moved, and her heart pounded at least three times for each one. She started forward again, but his arm went up across the doorway, blocking her path once more. Jolie fought the fear that was building steadily inside her, tugging at her flimsy controls.

"Jolie, if there's something wrong, you can tell me," he said softly.

"I need to get that call," she announced, as if he hadn't spoken at all. She trembled in spite of herself. "They probably need me back at the bank."

He was closer now, leaning into her. She felt his warm breath on her hair. "I'm very good at solving problems, Jolie."

She closed her eyes and sucked in a sharp breath as the remaining threads holding her together stretched even thinner. Images, voices, emotions all ran together inside her head. Her legs felt too weak to hold her up. She wanted to run, to hide, but didn't have the strength. Jolie could only stand there and pray she would wake up from this nightmare soon. Then, summoning every ounce of resolve she could, she forced her eyes open and manufactured the firmest glare she could aim in his direction. "Would you just let me through, please?"

"All right." He relented what seemed a lifetime later. "If you're certain there's nothing you want to talk about."

"I'm certain," she murmured.

Simon moved then, allowing her to pass. That she possessed the courage not to run like hell shocked her. But then, she couldn't run. For if she ran now, Simon Ruhl would know that she had something to hide. He would know her secret.

That she was just like her mother.

Chapter Four

Jolie stared at the gold-embossed business card in her hand as if by sheer willpower she could make something about the name and number printed there help make her remember.

And still nothing came.

The call from the bank hadn't been a big deal—just Renae letting Jolie know that her father had tried to reach her. It wasn't an emergency or anything; he simply wanted to touch base with her when she had time. For Jolie the call had been a bit untimely, but useful all the same. She'd transformed it into an excuse to avoid lunch with Simon Ruhl.

She glanced up from the card and surveyed the corridor outside her office and then the conference room across the hall. He was there. The conference room was now being used as an interview room and temporary office for him. Instantly, her palms started to sweat. He suspected her of something. She was sure of it.

But how could he?

Fear swelled in her throat, threatening to choke her. Did Renae suspect her, as well? Was Jolie the only one who hadn't known that something was very, very wrong? She'd resolved and covered up the most recent inconsistencies in her accounts. What if someone had noticed before she did so? Someone other than Renae. Simon Ruhl, maybe.

She tossed the card from the Cayman bank onto her desk and pushed to her feet. How could she have taken a trip and embezzled funds without remembering any of it?

The only possible answer was the worst case scenario.

She was losing her mind.

Mental illness.

It could be hereditary. She knew it could. She'd read all the articles about it. Her father warned her constantly about too much stress. Though he hadn't said it, he knew she was susceptible, more vulnerable than the average person. Jolie gritted her teeth. She'd been strong her entire life. Why did it have to start now? Her career had taken off earlier than expected. She could be bank president before reaching thirty-five. Why now?

Her mother's illness hadn't shown up until she was older. Then again, it could have been there all along, lying dormant just beneath the surface. Or maybe she'd started out like Jolie and kept it a secret, praying she could hang on to control. Hoping against hope that tomorrow would be better.

As if her troubling thoughts had somehow summoned him, Simon looked up. His gaze unerringly connected with hers. Jolie's breath stalled in her lungs and she ordered herself to turn and face the wall of windows that overlooked downtown Atlanta. She squeezed her eyes shut and banished his image, or at least attempted to. Her heart pounded harder and harder in her chest. She wanted to cry. Damn it. She blinked back tears. If she allowed them to fall it would be like surrendering…giving up…admitting defeat. She was confused enough without allowing this disturbing attraction to the man to get to her.

Drawing in a big, bolstering breath, she forced even the concept of surrender from her mind. She was not going to give up. Somehow she would sort out all this confusion, and this time she would maintain control. There would be no more slips, no blackouts. Whatever she had done in the past and couldn't remember was behind her. Her fingers curled instinctively into fists. From this moment on she would stay in complete control. Whatever it took, she would do it.

She swallowed back the rising lump of emotion. Yes, she could do it. Maybe she had made a mistake or two that she wasn't aware of, but it wouldn't happen again. No harm had been done to her clients. That was the most important thing in this whole mess. Everything was under control again—on the surface, anyway.

Forcing a calm that went only skin deep, Jolie turned back to her desk. Simon was watching. She didn't have to look up to know. She could feel his gaze on her. "Don't let him see you sweat," she mumbled as she riffled through the messages on her desk. "*Never* let the other side see you sweat." It was her father's philosophy and one she had adopted long ago. Losing her focus and revealing her fear would only give Simon Ruhl more leverage.

He already had too much.

"Got a minute?"

Startled, Jolie looked up to find Mark Boyer lounging in her open doorway. Frustration immediately lined her forehead. She did not want to lock horns with Mark this afternoon. She had too much on her mind already.

"Of course," she said, trying her level best to keep the tightness from her voice. It didn't work. The smirk on his face told her he'd picked up on the curtness in her tone.

He dropped into one of the chairs in front of her desk and crossed one leg over the other. "What's the deal with the brooding guy across the hall?" Mark jerked his head in the direction of the conference room.

Jolie moistened her lips and struggled for nonchalance. "You know why he's here as well as I do," she said flatly. "Mr. Knox explained that he's part of the in-house audit. Now, if you don't mind, I—"

Mark leaned forward and gave her one of those patronizing smiles that infuriated her. "Come on, Jolie, you don't have a minute for me anymore? What happened? I thought we were friends."

The promotion happened, Jolie thought, but didn't say it. He was the one who'd taken umbrage, and he had the nerve to behave as if the tension thickening between them was her fault? Fuming at the insinuation, she produced a smile of her own. "As difficult as you may find this to believe," she said, not caring now how short her tone was, "I have a great deal of work to do. It's nothing personal, Mark," she hastened to add. "Just business."

Just business. Those were the two words he had used the day the promotion had been announced. He'd been so sure the job was his that he'd gone on and on about how they shouldn't let the outcome change their relationship. "It's just business," he'd said. But he'd been singing a different tune when Jolie's name was announced.

For one long moment she was certain he intended to say what was really on his mind. The flicker of fury that showed briefly in those knowing blue eyes was nothing short of savage. But the moment passed as quickly as it came.

"Don't hesitate to let me know if you need any help," he offered, pushing himself to his feet. "We're still on the same team."

Jolie didn't relax until he was at the door again, poised to make his exit. When he paused and glanced back at her, she went on instant alert once more.

"I'm here for you, Jolie. Don't forget that if you need anything at all. I know how much stress is associated with this position. I only want to help."

And then he swaggered away, confident that he'd accomplished his mission.

Jolie's insides tightened into a thousand knots. The jerk had definitely accomplished his mission. He'd left her feeling exactly as he'd intended: inept.

SIMON PAID LITTLE HEED to Melba Scates as she spoke. His attention had shifted from the current employee interview to Jolie Randolph the moment Mark Boyer entered her office. Despite his best efforts, Simon's posture had gone rigid. He didn't like Boyer. He liked his blatant advances toward Jolie even less. Damn it! She was getting to him. Simon didn't relax again until Boyer had sauntered back to his own office. Simon refused to consider what that said about his objectivity.

Melba Scates droned on. Already well versed on the background of every single staff member employed by the bank, he didn't need to hear the lady's personal rendition. Jolie's obvious agitation held a great deal more interest for him.

Whatever she'd been searching for at her apartment had left her unnerved. Uncertain as to whether she had found it or not, Simon now felt quite positive about one thing: Jolie was running scared. He'd watched her from a distance for two solid weeks. Not once had he observed either her composure or her determination waver. *Relentless* would be the one word he would have used to describe her. Though her personal life left a lot to be desired and her social life verged on nonexistent, her professional focus went above and beyond the call of duty. He could see why she'd moved up the corporate ladder so quickly. Every move she made was toward one end—work.

Then, the night before last, everything had changed. She had had dinner with a friend and gone home with a stranger.

Simon's jaw clenched automatically when images from that night fell one over the other into his mind. He reminded himself again that Jolie was likely working for the enemy. An enemy he intended to bring down no matter the cost. He knew all too well how men like Raymond Brasco could lure unsuspecting innocents into a web of danger and deceit. Admittedly, Simon experienced some amount of sympathy for those caught in that trap. But the desire for vengeance he felt far outweighed any other emotion. He would stop Brasco this time, whatever the cost.

Just then Jolie tucked a handful of silky blond hair behind her ear, and something twisted deep inside Simon. He silently cursed himself for the weakness.

Refused to analyze it. Then exiled all emotion. He would allow nothing to stop him from his mission.

Raymond Brasco had set up shop in Atlanta more than fifteen years ago. The man had been too smart to get caught for a long time. Then a few years ago, Simon and his partner, Special Agent Tim Devers, had gotten close. Really close. But somehow, in his haste to make the bust of the decade, Simon had screwed up. A mere technicality in the search warrant had deemed the arrest invalid. Brasco had gone free and Simon had been reprimanded. Two days later Tim was executed by Brasco's men, leaving a wife and two small children behind. Simon knew Brasco was responsible. He also knew that it was punishment aimed directly at him for his cockiness when he'd arrested Brasco. He'd been so sure of himself...so sure that he'd covered all the bases. His overconfidence had cost Tim his life. Everyone told Simon he shouldn't blame himself. But how could he not? It was his fault. He had walked away from his career at the Bureau, but he'd sworn to himself that one day Brasco would pay.

That day was near.

Simon could feel it.

He would not make a mistake this time.

Nothing and no one would get in his way.

His gaze zeroed in on the woman across the hall, who had managed to get under his skin without even trying. Not even Jolie Randolph.

"And then I received the promotion to head teller," Melba Scates said, drawing Simon back to the here and now. She smiled proudly at him. "Is there anything else you'd like to know, Mr. Ruhl?"

Melba was a hard worker and as loyal as they

came. She was the mother of four and the grand-mother of ten. A single parent, she had put all four of her children through college on her salary combined with a weekend job. "That's fine, Ms. Scates." Simon produced an answering smile and stood, giving the kindly teller her cue to go. "If I think of anything else I'll let you know."

She nodded and followed him to the door.

"Thank you for your cooperation," he murmured, opening the door to facilitate her exit.

"You're quite welcome. Anything for the bank. It's my life," she said cheerfully.

Simon closed the door behind her and considered her parting words. He wondered if her children appreciated all the sacrifices she had made for them.

He had known even before he interviewed her that she could be crossed off the suspect list.

His gaze migrated to Jolie once more.

Too bad he couldn't say the same for her.

The cellular phone in his jacket pocket vibrated insistently. Simon had the volume muted so as not to interrupt his interviews.

"Simon Ruhl," he said in greeting.

"Good afternoon, Simon."

It took only those three words for Simon to know that his boss had been made aware of his failure to be completely forthcoming regarding his personal connection to this case.

"Victoria." He loosened his silk tie a centimeter or two and moved back behind the conference table turned desk.

"I received a call from an old friend of yours," she said, cutting straight to the point. "Cliff Medford."

Cliff and Simon had never been friends, but there was no need to bore Victoria with the distasteful details. Simon was reasonably certain Cliff had already presented his side of the story.

"Field Supervisor Medford," Simon clarified, in the event that his former superior had failed to mention that small detail.

"From the Birmingham, Alabama, office," Victoria added, allowing Simon to understand that she did, indeed, know.

Cliff had just made supervisor grade when the Brasco sting went down. He'd disliked Simon before that, and the bad bust had only made matters worse. As the senior agent on the case, Cliff had taken the fall along with Simon. Losing his assignment in Atlanta had turned Cliff's dislike to hatred. Obviously one of his old cronies in the Atlanta office had passed along the word that Simon was back in town and working a case that might have a connection to Brasco.

"And he told you," Simon added before Victoria bothered, "that I had a personal vendetta against Brasco."

"You know my feelings on an agent's personal involvement in a case," Victoria stated firmly. "However," she continued a bit less brusquely, "your word that any shared history between you and Brasco won't adversely affect this assignment is all I need."

Victoria was one of a kind. Simon had never met a woman quite like her. He respected her too much to lie to her. His deliberate omission when this assignment first came up had weighed heavily upon him, but his desire to do what had to be done had won in the end. Now that tactic seemed even more wrong than it had two weeks ago when Victoria offered him the case.

"You have my word." He would never take advantage of his position at the Colby Agency to the extent that it would jeopardize the case. She could rest assured of that fact.

"Then we don't have a problem. If things get sticky, Ian will bring in Max."

Max was an excellent choice. He would do the job every bit as well as Simon. But it wouldn't come to that. Simon would see to it.

"That won't be necessary at this point," he assured her. "Max would be my first choice as backup if the need arises."

"Very well. We'll wait for your call."

After the parting pleasantries were exchanged, Simon folded the cell phone and dropped it back into his pocket. Tamping down the fury that threatened his absolute control, he pressed the intercom button and waited for Renae to respond. The next employee on the list would get his mind off Cliff Medford and the real reason Simon had walked away from the Bureau. His failure to protect the innocent—his partner.

SITTING IN A COMFORTABLE, upholstered chair across the coffee table from Jolie, her best friend stared at her in silence for several beats before she spoke. The tension pressed in around them like a coming storm, making the air seem thick.

"You're sure you didn't know the guy?" Erica asked tentatively.

Jolie shook her head. Her stomach roiled each time

she recalled the moment she'd realized that she was in a stranger's bedroom...naked.

Erica took another sip of her chardonnay and then tipped her head to the right, an uncertain expression on her face. "Did you have...sex with him?"

For one long moment Jolie thought about lying, but this was Erica. They'd been best friends for nearly two years. Lying to her didn't seem right. And it wasn't as if her friend was overly conservative. Erica was a style unto herself. Hip and funky, yet chic, was the best way Jolie knew to describe her. She wore her short dark hair in a spiky do that was at once defiant and flattering. Her serious gray eyes were an utter contrast to her usual cocky expression. And she had one of those sexy moles near the corner of her mouth that completed the femme fatale picture.

"Honestly?" Jolie looked straight into her friend's expectant gaze. "I don't know." It sounded ridiculous, she knew, but it was the truth. "I woke up naked, so I can only assume..." She splayed her hands in doubt. "I'm reasonably sure that if we did he used a condom. There was no..." She shrugged.

Erica nodded solemnly. "That's good news."

Leaning more fully against the sofa back, Jolie pulled her knees up under her chin. She felt exhausted. When she'd come home all she could think about was climbing into the shower and then going to bed, but Erica had called to say she'd made it back, and Jolie had convinced her to come over for a glass of wine. She had to find out if her friend knew anything that would help her solve the mystery of night before last.

"You're sure I didn't talk to anyone or mention someone I planned to meet?"

Erica shook her head. "We met at the restaurant after work. We had a great dinner, but I had to cut out early, since my flight was practically at dawn the next morning. You said you wanted to hang out awhile." Erica chewed her lower lip as she searched her memory. "You'd driven over and seemed perfectly capable of driving yourself home. One or two glasses of wine were all you'd had. We go to Carlisle's all the time. It's an upscale establishment. There was no reason not to think you'd be safe there."

"It's not your fault. Don't you dare even think that!" Jolie frowned as she considered another detail, adding an additional amount of tension to her throbbing skull. "But my car was at home the next morning."

Still looking as if she blamed herself, Erica calculated that fact into the equation. "Then maybe you left the restaurant alone." Her expression brightened as if she were onto something. "What if the guy met you at your house? You know, someone you've been out with before."

Jolie shook her head wearily. "But that still doesn't explain why I can't remember anything."

Erica remained silent this time, but the worry in her eyes told Jolie exactly what she was thinking: drugs.

"I should have gone straight to a hospital and had myself tested," Jolie admitted in hindsight. "Then I would know."

Erica nodded in agreement. "Maybe it's not too late?" she suggested thoughtfully. "Some drugs stay in your system longer than others, don't they?"

Jolie shrugged, then sighed in defeat. What difference did it make? She didn't even know the guy's name. She'd been so out of it that morning when she ran from his apartment that she hadn't even been able to recall the address later in the day, when all the possible repercussions had come crashing in on her.

"I can't even remember where his apartment was. Even if I knew he'd drugged me, I couldn't press charges because I don't know who he is."

Erica set her glass aside and moved to the edge of the seat. "What if we just drive around until you see something that looks familiar? I mean, surely you'd recognize the place if you saw it."

Jolie thought about that for a moment. The room had been luxurious. That narrowed things down fractionally. She had arrived at the office less than one hour late that morning. Since she'd taken the time to shower and change, that meant that the stranger's apartment couldn't have been more than half an hour from her place, considering the time she'd actually arrived at work.

"We could try, I suppose." Jolie relaxed marginally. But what would that accomplish? Maybe she should just put the whole incident out of her mind and get on with her life. What good would knowing do her?

Erica moved to the sofa next to Jolie. "Look," she said soothingly, "if you want to just forget it, then let's do that. At least for a while. We don't have to pursue this right now."

Jolie gifted her friend with a watery smile. This was what she'd needed tonight. A friend who cared. "Thanks."

Erica hugged her quickly, then drew back and wiped her own tears away. "This is an awful reality to face. But if you really believe he used a condom, maybe you're safe. Did you make an appointment with your gynecologist?''

Jolie nodded. She had done that. Though she couldn't get in for another week, at least she would feel better when she'd been thoroughly checked out.

''Here.'' Erica handed her the stemmed glass still half-full of Jolie's favorite chardonnay. ''Drink. It'll calm you down.''

Jolie did as instructed, draining the glass in one long gulp, though she doubted it would help as much as Erica seemed to think.

Erica freshened both glasses and moved back to the chair opposite the sofa. They sat in relieved silence for a long while. Jolie was thankful for the reprieve, though she had scarcely scratched the surface of what was bothering her. There was more she needed to share with her friend. As if reading her mind, Erica asked, ''What is it you're not telling me?''

Jolie looked away. This part should be easier, after confessing to her night with a stranger, but oddly, it wasn't. ''There have been some inconsistencies in several of my accounts at the bank.''

Erica searched her eyes for what felt like forever before commenting. ''You're certain they're your inconsistencies?''

Jolie nodded. ''Somehow I set up an account at a Cayman bank and—''

''When you say Cayman,'' Erica interrupted, clearly startled, ''you mean as in the Cayman Islands?''

Jolie nodded again. ''Apparently I've been siphoning off money from some of my clients' accounts and depositing them in my own secret account.''

To say her friend looked shocked would be a colossal understatement. "You mean that you accidentally put money in the wrong account, right?"

Jolie shook her head. "I flew to Grand Cayman, set up an account and started making deposits from ongoing accounts. You know, the kind clients get a statement about only every six months or so. Since I just started doing it three months ago, no one's noticed."

Erica held up both hands. "You're freaking me out here, Jolie. You're telling me that you deliberately set out to embezzle from your bank?"

Again, Jolie responded with a wag of her head. "I don't remember doing it, so you can't really call it deliberate." She reached behind the throw pillow next to her and pulled out the T-shirt with the island scene depicted upon it. "I bought this on my credit card in a George Town shop while I was there three months ago. I have no recollection whatsoever of the trip, much less the purchase."

Erica's frown deepened. "You didn't mention taking a trip. When did this supposedly happen?"

Jolie furnished the details. Like hers, Erica's confusion and disbelief mounted as the incredible tale unfolded.

Then something must have dawned on Erica, for she caught her breath.

"What?" Jolie couldn't tolerate the suspense. "What did you remember?"

"That was the weekend I had the flu." Her gaze connected with Jolie's. "Remember, my mother had to come and stay the weekend with me? I tried to call you but..."

She didn't have to finish the statement. Jolie knew the rest. She hadn't been home.

Dread roiled deep in her belly. "You know what this means."

Erica didn't say a word, but Jolie read the answer in her eyes. It was the same conclusion she'd already reached.

She was just like her mother.

She was slowly losing her grip on reality.

When Erica had reluctantly gone home for the evening, Jolie carefully placed their wineglasses in the sink. She poured the last of the chardonnay down the drain and set the bottle aside. She should call her father. She had to tell him…in case intervention was necessary.

What was she thinking? It was already necessary. She'd lost it. She was not only mentally unstable, she was a criminal!

Tears burned behind her tightly clenched eyelids. Dear God. What on earth was she going to do?

The doorbell rang, almost shattering the last of her control.

Swiping back the stream of tears, Jolie moved toward the front door. Erica hadn't wanted to leave her. She'd probably decided to turn around and come back. She was a good friend.

Without bothering to check the peephole Jolie jerked the door open. "Coming back wasn't necessary. I—" She lost her voice abruptly when her gaze collided with an intense dark one that did not belong to Erica.

"You seemed upset when you left the bank today. I thought perhaps I should check on you. May I come in?"

Simon Ruhl looking as dark and alluring—not to mention dangerous—as always waited patiently for her to regain her ability to speak. He still wore the black designer suit with its matching black shirt and silk tie that he'd worn at the bank today, yet not a single wrinkle marred the elegance.

"I'm fine," she finally managed to blurt. The disorientation she'd suffered briefly when her gaze connected with his quickly transformed into annoyance. Why was he hounding her? Wasn't it enough that she had to deal with his presence at work? "I appreciate your stopping by, but it wasn't necessary."

The intensity of that penetrating gaze only increased with her attempts to put him off. "You're sure about that?"

Her temper flaring just enough to chase away any lingering trepidation, she planted one hand on her hip and glared at him. "Mr. Ruhl, your persistence is bordering on harassment. So far I've resisted tossing out accusations like that, but you appear determined to force my hand."

He didn't smile, but she could have sworn she saw a slight twitch in those full lips of his, which only added to her fury.

"I can assure you, Miss Randolph, that my curiosity as to your well-being is strictly professional. I'm not one to break the rules. You did share a number of concerns with me at our first meeting."

Renewed humiliation rushed through her. "You're right, I did. But that was before, this is now. If you don't mind, I'm off duty. This is my private time and I don't appreciate your interference." She stepped back to close the door. "I'll see you at the bank in the morning."

One broad palm flattened against the door when she would have closed it in his face. "I hope you'll accept my apology for overstepping my bounds," he offered with absolutely no hint of genuine sincerity.

If allowing him to believe that all was well would send him on his way, she was all for it. "Certainly." She forced a smile. "Good night, Mr. Ruhl."

"Sleep well, Miss Randolph."

He stared deeply into her eyes for three long beats before turning away. Only when the door was closed and locked between them did Jolie feel secure again.

But it was only temporary.

Tomorrow she would have to face him once more.

But for now she had other worries…like getting through the night without doing something she wouldn't remember come morning.

Chapter Five

She loved this room.

Jolie sighed as she relaxed into a leather tufted side chair near her father's massive desk. His study had always been like a sanctuary to her. She'd felt close to him there. This had been the place where he'd spent most of his time when he was home from the office. Playing in here had been forbidden, but Jolie had always managed to do just that. Whenever her mother had lapsed into one of her moods or disappeared for a day or two, Jolie had found solace in her father's study. Work had kept him at the office more nights than she cared to remember. But here, in this room, she had felt as if a part of him was always there.

The room epitomized all that her father stood for. The heavy furnishings and ornate design details spoke of strength and dependability. Despite the masculine decor, a subtle elegance could be found in the softer touches about the room, like the fresh cut flowers that graced the table between the two chairs adjacent to his desk. Or the grand portrait of Jolie at age eighteen that hung over the exquisitely detailed mahogany credenza beyond his desk. A small brass-bordered photograph of her mother sat amid a collage of framed family moments on the glossy surface of the credenza.

Though she was no longer a child, after a week of dealing with Simon Ruhl, Jolie definitely needed a sanctuary. She closed her eyes and inhaled deeply of the familiar scents of her childhood. The lemony smell of the polish that Vera, the housekeeper, used to clean the elegant mahogany furnishings. The vaguest hint of cherry pipe tobacco from which her father had probably sneaked a puff or two quite recently. The gentle fragrance of fresh cut daisies, snapdragons, mums and greens that at once sweetened the air and underscored the deeper, more androcentric aromas of richly oiled wood and butter soft leather.

A smile slid over her lips as she considered that he'd probably ordered the fresh flowers specifically to mask the lingering odor of tobacco before Friday morning coffee with his daughter. Months ago the doctor had ordered him to stop indulging in his half-century-old habit. Obviously her dad hadn't paid full heed, and Jolie intended to bring that little detail to his attention. Franklin Randolph was a man who allowed few self-gratifications other than the occasional cocktail and his beloved evening session with his favorite pipe. But hypertension would not be ignored. Nor would his daughter, she decided right then and there. He certainly stayed on her case frequently enough. Closer to seventy than sixty, her father professed that he was now paying for years of high pressure decisions and eighty-hour work weeks. He warned her repeatedly that she was headed down the same path. Too much stress was a very bad thing, he would say.

For the first time in her adult life Jolie felt ready

to admit he'd been right all along. If he only knew just how right. She swallowed, forcing down a rising lump of unfamiliar emotion. Personal defeat had been a stranger to her as an adult…until now.

Jolie's lids drifted open as she caught a whiff of decadent coffee. A sense of safety cloaked her and the weight of oppression lifted just a little as her father entered the study carrying a laden silver tray. For now, right here, nothing could touch her. She was safe.

"Here we go." He placed the tray on the table next to the flowers. "Tell me," he said as he proceeded to pour the steaming brew, "what has put those unsightly circles under your lovely green eyes?" He smiled down at Jolie as he offered her a delicate china cup and saucer. The china had been in her mother's family for three generations. One day, her father told her on a regular basis, it would belong to Jolie. "You promised you'd stop putting in so many hours once you were settled in the new position," he reminded her firmly.

Taking the seat opposite her, he reached for the remaining cup and saucer, then waited silently for her to vent. It was a weekly ritual. If she had any complaints about the bank or any of her peers, she admitted so only to her father. He was her sounding board. Someone to whom she could admit most anything and be assured it would go no further.

But this was different.

Buying time before she began, she sipped the rich, warm gourmet blend her father had prepared, and reveled in the robust flavor. Friday morning coffee with her father was like having her own private therapy session. Having retired as bank president of that very institution, he understood every aspect of her work, good and bad. On Fridays between 7:30 and 8:30 a.m. they were no longer father and daughter, but colleagues who shared a mutual respect not only for each other, but also for the ever changing and intriguing world of domestic and international banking.

"It's not the number of hours I'm putting in," she protested thoughtfully. "It's this new member of the audit team." The statement was true, to an extent.

Her father lifted one gray brow in a skeptical manner. "New member?"

She nodded, the image of Simon Ruhl immediately blooming life-size amid her thoughts. "Apparently Mr. Hodges wanted more than the routine drill. He requested in-depth personnel reviews as well. A Mr. Simon Ruhl is conducting the proceedings."

The frown that furrowed her father's brow reflected her own feelings of confusion regarding the matter. Annual audits were as routine as cleaning teeth. Generally the only time personnel were investigated was when someone was suspected of wrongdoing or major discrepancies had been discovered. Therein lay the crux of her anxiety.

Fear knotted her stomach, abruptly ruining her enjoyment of the delicious coffee. Had other discrepancies—ones she or Renae hadn't noticed—been found in her accounts? What if this whole exercise was about her? She'd watched Simon with the other employees, and it was clear that his major focus remained on her. With more certainty than she cared to confess even to herself, she knew he suspected her of wrongdoing. Ice slid through her veins, sending a tremor all the way to her fingertips. Fine, irreplaceable china rattled before she could stem the quaking in her limbs.

"Heightened protective measures have trickled down to financial institutions as a matter of homeland security," her father suggested. "I'm certain we'll see more additional safeguards as time goes on." He took a generous sip of coffee. "In fact," he added, "I would be more concerned if increased checks were not put into place." The frown reappeared above his hazel eyes. "Is there some reason this step disturbs you?"

Jolie had never lied to her father, not even back in high school when it was the cool thing to do. The ice still clogging her veins was chilling her bones now. How could she tell him what she suspected about herself? About the inconsistencies in her accounts that Renae had come across? About the travel voucher to the Cayman Islands?

Dear God, how could she explain that she had awakened naked and disoriented in a stranger's bed?

She couldn't.

The band of dread tightened around her chest, making it difficult to breathe.

If she told him, he would know that the symptoms had begun. He would know that she was just like her mother.

Jolie's gaze flew to the proudly displayed photograph of her mother in happier days. She'd been the perfect wife, the perfect mother—a member of the PTA at school, a prominent and well-respected member of numerous women's clubs in the community. Then, out of the blue, life as the Randolphs knew it had changed. It had taken years for Jolie and her father to come to terms with the disease and then the loss. Eventually they both had learned to remember the good times and forget the bad. It had worked…to a degree.

And now it was starting all over again.

"No," Jolie lied in answer to her father's question. "There's no particular reason. I…I just thought the step somewhat odd. Even the department heads were given no real warning. Mr. Ruhl simply appeared one day. The move was so unlike Mr. Hodges or the board of directors." She shook her head. "Something doesn't feel right about it."

Her father considered that last statement for a moment, as if deciding whether he believed her response, or perhaps attempting to determine if he recognized the man who currently served as the bane of her existence at work. For four days Simon had haunted her at the office, even boldly showing up at her door, on Tuesday night. He watched her every move, sifted through her work, touching the documents she had drawn up as if they possessed some secret knowledge of her. She moistened her lips and swallowed in an effort to dampen her dry throat. It didn't help. Simon Ruhl frightened her more than any man she had ever known, yet he drew her on a level that was beyond control…beyond all reason.

Sure, he was attractive, tall and dark, but his magnetism amounted to far more than mere aesthetics. There was an alluring charm about him that bordered somehow on dangerous, but drew her as nothing else ever had. He was like the boy every mother warned her daughters about, the one who broke hearts and stole virtues. Only Simon was better dressed and more intelligent.

"If instinct tells you something is out of sync, then

it probably is,'' her father offered. "Jason Hodges is no fool, nor are any of the members of his board. If he suspects something is amiss, he will attempt to intercede before it becomes a larger issue, perhaps out of his jurisdiction.''

Jolie shivered before she could stop herself. This time she set her cup and saucer aside, hoping to disguise the trembling of her hands by folding them in her lap.

"Jolie," her father said, stepping back into the role of father with a mere fluctuation in the nuances of his deep voice, "are you certain these concerns troubling you are related to work?''

She met his gaze, praying that she could ask what had to be asked and still keep it together. "Dad, how old was mother when her first symptom of mental illness manifested itself?''

IT HAPPENED EVERY TIME she asked about her mother's illness. Her father behaved exactly the same way: he became incensed. He would always insist that her mother's situation had nothing to do with Jolie.

Jolie gritted her teeth as she parked her car in the bank's parking garage. But that wasn't true. She had done her research. Her mother's illness could be hereditary. She didn't want to make her father relive the hurt; all she needed were a few simple answers. What was the first sign that something was wrong? Had her mother appeared normal between episodes? Had her condition deteriorated as quickly as Jolie recalled?

Her father would say nothing except that what had happened to her mother had no bearing on the present. Jolie was not her mother. He did not want to rehash that painful past.

Emerging from the car, she blinked back the tears stinging her eyes. She'd come so close to telling him about the money and the Cayman account. The words had gathered in her throat, expanding like a scream, but she'd held them back, too afraid that the admission would make them even more real.

Terror fisted in her gut. Dear God, it was real.

She couldn't think about this anymore this morning. She'd lose all control if she didn't stop now. Gathering her courage around her like a shield, Jolie cleared her throat, squared her shoulders and entered the bank with the best smile she could summon.

"Good morning, Miss Randolph," Henry, the security guard, said as he closed and relocked the door behind her.

"Good morning, Henry. Isn't your granddaughter's birthday this weekend?"

Henry grinned proudly. "Yes, ma'am. She'll be seven. The wife has a big bash planned. You should stop by."

"I'll do my best," Jolie promised, before rushing toward the stairs and her office. Henry and his wife were raising their granddaughter, as so many grandparents were these days. Their one and only daughter had refused to marry the father of the child, and had eventually left the child in the custody of her parents so she could go back to college. It wasn't that she was a bad person, she'd simply been too young to realize the consequences of her actions and the ultimate responsibility of her decisions.

Jolie paused on the second story landing to take a final glance down at the gallery. The sight never failed to soothe her. The tellers busily prepared for opening, their movements efficient and unconsciously synchronized. Henry monitored the side door closest to the parking garage to facilitate the entry of the bank's many staff members. Another guard, one whom Jolie recognized, but did not know personally, stood ready to open the front door the moment the grand clock hanging on the wall above the teller counter reached 9:00 a.m. It was Friday morning; for the bank, rush hour would last all day. Most of their customers were paid on Friday and even those who weren't needed a cash infusion before the weekend.

Jolie sighed, thankful for the moment of ordinary bliss. Just then Henry opened the door once more and Simon Ruhl entered. He paused and took a moment to take stock of his surroundings, his gaze going straight to her as if he sensed her presence on the landing above him.

For several seconds she couldn't move. She could only stand there and permit those penetrating eyes to stare straight into her soul. His intensity was palpable. She could feel him reaching out to her, the connection deeper than any she'd ever experienced.

"Miss Randolph, there's a call for you."

Renae's voice jerked Jolie from the trance she'd slipped into, leaving her weak-kneed and feeling more empty than she'd ever felt in her life.

"Coming," she managed to answer, before her assistant, offering a quick smile, hurried off to her own office with a stack of files in hand.

Refusing to take one last look down at the gallery, Jolie shook off the troubling sensations and put one foot in front of the other, determinedly making the trip to her office. She would not let Simon get to her already. She had work to do. At least for a little while she had to put everything else out of her mind.

Jolie dropped her briefcase onto her credenza and turned to the phone on her desk. This was what she did, who she was. Maybe her father was right. Maybe she was simply letting the stress get to her. Probably she'd eventually find a reasonable explanation for everything that had happened—including the Cayman bank account. She couldn't possibly have done such a thing.

Feeling more sure of herself than she had all week, Jolie lifted the receiver and pressed the blinking button. "Jolie Randolph."

"I've missed you, Jolie."

The voice was male...deep and somehow familiar. Jolie's breath abandoned her. "Who is this?" she heard herself ask, her voice weak with fear and uncertainty. Her heart stumbled into a faster rhythm, sending that fear and uncertainly pumping through her like the poison from a lethal injection.

He laughed softly. "Don't play games with me, Jolie. I think you know who I am."

She moistened her lips and tightened her free hand into a fist for courage. "You shouldn't call me at work," she said more firmly, allowing him to believe she had indeed recognized him. She abruptly remembered the call Renae had taken on Monday, from an unidentified man who had wanted to know if she had made it to work. This man. The one with whom she'd likely spent the night. Well, he was wrong. She had no intention of playing games. "If you'll excuse me, I'm very busy right now."

"Don't pretend you don't remember last weekend," the voice urged before she could hang up. "I know I won't ever forget our special time together."

Fury seared her, evaporating all other emotion. "What do you want?"

"You." A definitive click punctuated the answer. The voice was gone.

Struggling to regain her composure, Jolie slowly lowered the receiver back to its cradle. She closed her eyes and forced away the urge to scream. Even in her angst she felt the subtle shift in the atmosphere around her that signaled the bank doors had been opened for business. At that very moment the usual Friday morning crowd was pouring into the lobby below, ready for business as usual. Jolie opened her eyes and dragged in a deep breath. She held it to the count of five and slowly released it. She had to relax and at the same time get a grip on her composure. No matter what he said, she didn't know the man or the voice on the phone. Yes, it had sounded vaguely familiar, but she heard dozens of voices every day in the bank. It could be anyone. As if to refute her protests, the image of the naked stranger in his shower loomed large in her mind.

No matter how hard she tried to rationalize it, she couldn't deny that it had happened and that there was no rational explanation for her behavior. The truth was she didn't know what was going on. She wasn't sure of anything anymore. And she was certain that no matter how long she searched, she would never find a simple explanation for the events that had taken place recently in her life. There would be no mere misunderstanding, no mistaken identity.

Jolie was guilty.

The only thing she could hope to discover was the true extent of her transgression.

SIMON MADE HIS ROUNDS at the bank, offering hellos and answering questions from those who still felt ill at ease in his presence. He felt confident that most of the employees were innocent of any wrongdoing. However, that did not stop those who had allowed even the passing fantasy of taking some of the bank's money for themselves from feeling guilty when they had to look him in the eye. It was instinctive. He imagined that years of fire and brimstone sermons every Sunday morning had engrained the wrongness of even a sinful thought.

As he entered the conference room he looked out over the bank's lobby. The view was almost as good as the Atlanta skyline from the outer offices. The large, marble-floored gallery and intricately detailed woodwork below was reminiscent of another era. The cold, austere design of newer office buildings was no match for this kind of inviting luxury.

But it was the other view, the one directly across the corridor, that made him appreciate using this room as an office. His gaze sought Jolie. She wore a pale yellow skirt with a matching jacket this morning. Like everything else in her wardrobe, it fitted her petite figure as if it had been tailored specifically for her. As he watched she peeled off the jacket, revealing a silky white sleeveless blouse that hugged gentle curves. Before he could stop himself, his gaze roamed the length of her shapely legs as she moved across the room to hang up her jacket. His body tensed with the attraction that had been building all week. He laughed softly, disgustedly at that understatement. The desire had been there from the beginning. From the moment he'd first seen Jolie Randolph from behind the concealing tint of his car window he'd wanted her on a physical level. The attraction had been instant and savage. It was anything but fleeting…anything but uncomplicated.

At thirty-five, Simon had had his share of physical relationships, had even been close to marriage once. It wasn't like he didn't know the score when it came to this sort of thing. He had never allowed personal feelings to interfere with an investigation, but somehow this time he appeared to have no control over the matter. Jolie occupied his every thought. He looked away and shook his head. She'd even invaded his dreams, which was definitely a first.

As ridiculous as it seemed, he had to keep reminding himself that she was his prime suspect—one of them, anyway. Her longtime associate and friend, Mark Boyer, was the other.

Simon directed his focus to the stack of employee files before him. He would not permit this foolish attraction to develop further. He had a job to do. For the first time he had the opportunity to set to rights the wrong that had taken the life of his partner. Nothing—his gaze shifted to Jolie once more—was going to stop him from making that happen.

Like a number of others employed here, Jolie felt uneasy whenever Simon questioned her. But her guilt was different. Though he still had misgivings regarding the extent of her actual involvement in the money laundering the Bureau suspected, she was mixed up in it somehow. He felt it with every fiber of his being, and he was seldom wrong.

Jolie Randolph knew something, played some part in Raymond Brasco's scheme. All Simon had to do was figure out the role she played. On a very real level she was completely innocent; he couldn't deny that. His assumption was instinct, pure and simple. He knew innocence when he encountered it, the same as he recognized deceit. Though Jolie had not met with Brasco or any of his people during the time Simon had been watching her, there was still the possibility that a covert meeting had taken place at some point. Simon had divided much of his time between watching Jolie and observing Boyer's activities. But it was Jolie who would provide the evidence, Simon was certain. Boyer was too smart…too careful. Jolie acted on emotion. She was the weak link in whatever was going on.

When she broke, Simon would be there. He shoved away the files on the table before him and swore softly at his own stupidity. Though he told himself repeatedly he would be there to take her down, the truth was he wanted to be there to protect her, as well. Yes, he wanted to uncover the connection. He needed to discover any and all evidence related to Brasco's activities. But some ridiculously chivalrous part of him that he couldn't put aside wanted to save her.

He wanted to save her from herself.

Chapter Six

Five o'clock couldn't come quickly enough for Jolie.
The atmosphere at the bank had been uncharacteristically tense all day, and that was saying something,
considering the week she'd had. As was par for the
course, Simon Ruhl appeared at every turn. Even
when she shut herself up in her own office he was
there, right across the hall, watching her. She'd lost
count of the times she'd caught him staring at her.
What was worse, he didn't even bother looking away
when she noticed his unabashed behavior.

His eyes—those dark-as-midnight pools of pure
temptation—bored right through her. She shivered at
the mere thought of how he openly undressed her
with his gaze, studied her as if she were a species he
had never before encountered.

She'd tried to mollify herself with the possibility
that he might simply be attracted to her. That would
certainly be better than the alternative. But Jolie was
sure it was something more than plain old lust. He
observed her every move far too closely for his intentions to be purely sexual.

No, she was very nearly convinced that he intended
not only to unnerve her, but to keep her that way.

Wanted her off balance so that he could catch her doing something wrong…something illegal.

Jolie swallowed tightly as she packed up to go home for the day. Well, she had intentions of her own. Her first priority was to ensure that all of her accounts and records stayed in perfect order, now that she had them that way. Second, she had settled on a method to try and keep track of her own moves. She snatched up her journal and shoved it into her purse. Foolish as it sounded, she now kept a precise log of her comings and goings as well as her every transaction at work, including dates and times. She made note of when she awoke and when she went to bed at night. If another blackout occurred she would at least have some sort of time line by which to determine when and where she'd last been herself.

Slinging her bag over her shoulder, Jolie headed out of her office. It seemed incredible that at twenty-eight years of age she found such desperate measures necessary. That another blackout might never occur was a possibility, but she wasn't willing to chance it. She would not sit back and allow herself to become as helpless as her mother had grown in those last months of her life.

Careful not to look toward the conference room as she moved away from her office door, Jolie exchanged pleasantries about the weekend with several of her co-workers, including Renae. Forty-eight hours without Simon Ruhl underfoot would be a blessing. Her nerves were raw from continued exposure to the man and the paradox he represented to her emotions. One second she wanted to have wild, hot sex with him and the next she wanted to run for her life.

Maybe her mental condition was already far worse

than she suspected. She had to be out of her mind to be thinking about anything remotely pleasurable when it came to him. He was the proverbial thorn in her side.

As she emerged into the September evening she felt a sense of relief despite the lingering heat and humidity of the day. She was free. Dinner with her best friend seemed a perfect way to celebrate. Erica had wanted to have lunch with her, but Jolie's day had been too booked with meetings for her to leave the office. Probably her friend wanted to see if she was still holding it together. After all, Jolie had told her everything. Considering what that entailed, she was surprised Erica hadn't ordered the guys in the little white coats to come and take Jolie away. Certainly her father would have done just that had she been as forthcoming with him. She loved her father immensely, but he preferred to sweep the past under the rug, pretend it never happened. *You're fine, Jolie. Everything is fine, Jolie. What happened to your mother has nothing to do with anything.*

But everything wasn't fine. She started her car and pulled away from her designated parking slot in the massive garage. She had a very bad feeling that things would never be *fine* again.

SIMON WATCHED, his tension mounting with each passing second. He had followed Jolie home, then returned to the bank, since Boyer had opted to stay late on a Friday evening, something he had not done in the past three weeks. Simon had recently gained authorization to bug the offices, and had listened as Boyer straightened up his work space. When he'd completed the task, he'd left, dropped by a video rental store and picked up two of the most recent releases and driven home. Within thirty minutes three other vehicles had arrived, as well as a pizza delivery.

Calling in the license plates to an old friend still serving at the local Bureau office, Simon had learned that Boyer's guests were some of his colleagues from other financial institutions around Atlanta. None had any known ties to Brasco. Satisfied that Boyer was in for the evening, Simon had then driven to Jolie's residence and set up watch.

Her decision to take a long, hot bath was the reason for his rigid muscles at the moment. He'd managed to leave a tracking device as well as a transmitter in the form of an ink pen in her purse today. She had apparently turned her purse upside down in the bathroom, spilling out the contents. The reception was entirely too clear now. Under normal conditions he would have been thankful, but not tonight.

He'd watched her move about the apartment, seen her silhouette against the sheer drapes and, at times, her image through a large curtained window. The window in the master bath was shuttered, but he'd heard every move she made. The loud splashing as water filled the tub. The phone ringing in the background, a call she'd chosen not to answer. After four rings her answering machine had picked up, but the voice of whoever called had been drowned out by the rushing water. He'd imagined the billowing steam rising, fragrant with the jasmine he smelled on her skin.

As if his own imagination wasn't providing enough erotic temptation, the water had stopped and then had come a tiny sigh of relief as she'd slipped off her strappy high-heeled sandals. The whisper of silky, feminine fabric as she'd undressed. He'd heard the barely perceptible rasp of the brush as she'd dragged it through her hair, probably twisting it up out of the way in some casual fashion. Then, the straw that had broken the camel's back, the soft throaty sounds of her appreciation as she'd slipped into the swirling, heated water. His too vivid mind had conjured the vision of them making love, and those sounds echoing from her as he stroked her skin and then plunged deeper and deeper into her.

He gripped the steering wheel, waiting for the need to pass and for his body to relax once more. But long minutes later even the guileless sounds of her deep, even breaths made him want her more. He'd watched her all week, stolen every possible moment to stand too close or lean even nearer. He had ensured that their hands touched frequently, their shoulders brushed at every opportunity. He'd heard her breath catch each time. Hard as she'd tried, she was not unaffected herself. There was a definite attraction between them. He'd told himself that he was using that unexpected chemistry to his advantage. Assured himself that keeping her off balance was worth whatever it cost him on a personal level...that *he* could keep his head on straight.

But now he had his doubts about those lofty assurances. His body as well as his mind was very much involved in this forbidden fantasy. However much he wished it not to be, it was. Jolie Randolph had crept so deeply under his skin he couldn't be certain of his motives anymore.

He clenched his jaw in denial. His motives had not changed. He would do what he'd set out to. Raymond Brasco's empire was about to come crashing down. Jolie was nothing but a means to an end. The fact that

Simon wanted to make love to her had nothing to do with anything. If getting what he wanted required a performance between the sheets, he would be happy to oblige.

But it would alter nothing.

The subtle change in her respiration and then the sound of sloshing water jerked Simon's attention back to the present.

He blocked the images that accompanied the sounds. He was in too deep now. Even he wasn't so blind or stubborn as to not realize when he was headed into dangerous waters.

Danger had never stopped him before. In fact, it had more times than not been an ally. This time would prove no different, he affirmed. He could handle it. All he had to do was focus.

JOLIE STEPPED FROM the tub and wrapped a generous bath towel around her damp skin. The water had felt wonderful, had relaxed her completely. She'd spent an hour walking the floors when she hadn't been able to reach Erica. But a long hot bath had eased her frazzled nerves. After toweling dry, she pulled on a chenille robe and made her way to the kitchen. She hadn't eaten right in days. Her tummy rumbled now, protesting her neglect.

A quick scan of the instructions and she popped a frozen dinner into the microwave. While it nuked she padded out to the entry hall and checked the answering machine. She'd heard the phone ring as she'd prepared for her bath, but she'd needed the bath a great deal more than she'd needed to talk. It could have been Erica, though, so she pressed the play button to hear the message the caller had left.

"Jolie."

The voice.

She trembled. The male voice from the phone this morning. Vaguely familiar, yet completely alien. Hard as she tried she could not put a face to the voice.

"I've missed you...please don't keep me waiting any longer." A pause. Her heart thundered so hard she could scarcely catch her breath. "I'll be waiting tonight at the Blue Parrot. Don't disappoint me."

A click and then a dial tone told her the message had ended even before the computerized voice recited the date and time.

The Blue Parrot.

She chewed her lower lip and searched her memory banks for any recognition. A club, she reasoned. Dragging out the Yellow Pages, she quickly thumbed to the right section. Her finger slid down the page until she found the name she sought. The Blue Parrot was a jazz club downtown. She'd never been there before, she was fairly certain. Dredging the recesses of her mind, she shoved the Yellow Pages back onto the shelf beneath the phone and tried to think if maybe she'd been there with friends and simply forgotten. She shook her head. Nope. She was positive she'd never been to that particular club. Truth was, she didn't have much of a social life. Other than a rare dinner with friends, she hardly did anything other than work and sleep.

An unexpected sadness tugged at her. How had she allowed her life to become so consumed with work? She'd dated in high school and in college. What had happened to change the well-balanced woman she used to be? The promise of promotion. She sighed and plowed her fingers through her damp hair. Mr.

Knox had dangled one promotion after the other in front of her, insisting that he saw something in her that one rarely found in an executive so young. He'd urged and encouraged her to strive for that next rung on the career ladder until it had become an addiction…an obsession.

Jolie hugged herself as that realization vibrated through her. How could it suddenly be so clear? How could she not have seen herself slipping over the edge of obsession? God, she'd turned into a regular Type A—all work and no play.

No wonder she didn't have a life. She'd spent the past five years pushing everyone away so that she could focus solely on work. Maybe that's why her father hounded her all the time. Why hadn't she seen that before now?

Because you never see it until it's too late, a little voice told her. She shivered, hugging herself more tightly. She thought of the blackouts, of the bizarre account at an overseas bank with her name on it, and then of the seductive voice on the answering machine. Was it too late? Could she really have done all these things and have absolutely no recall of any of it?

She shook her head, denying that possibility. It just couldn't be. A sane person would never forget such monumental steps. Perhaps that was the key: sane. It all went back to her mother's illness. The one she'd obviously inherited.

Jolie shook her head again. She would not accept that fate. She was stronger than that. When she would have turned back to the kitchen, a flash of blue grabbed her troubled attention. Her gaze swung to the basket next to the telephone where she usually tossed her keys. Her keys were there. She remembered dropping them in it on her way in this evening. But there was something else, some inner instinct telling her this was not good. She reached cautiously toward the basket. Her heart picked up its pace once more, the blood rushing in her ears rendering her deaf. With her right hand she plucked the item from the basket, then studied it as renewed horror mushroomed inside her.

A book of matches. The kind one picked up at a bar or nightclub. The Blue Parrot logo was printed on the cover. This couldn't be. She'd never been to that club before. She didn't even smoke, so why would she have picked up a book of matches? She looked inside the flap just in case someone had written a number there, but it was blank.

She pressed the play button on her answering machine once more and listened to the voice. He would be waiting. *Don't disappoint me.* She looked at the matchbook in her hand. If she went there, would she recognize him? Would the memories all come flooding back? Could he—would he—fill in the blanks she could not account for?

She had to know.

She couldn't live another minute like this.

AT JUST PAST 8:00 p.m., Simon was surprised to see Jolie leave her apartment and climb into her car. Maybe this was the break he'd been waiting for. He knew she'd played back the telephone message she'd received, but since the transmitter was still in the bathroom, he hadn't been able to distinguish the words spoken. Unfortunately, she'd accessorized with another, smaller handbag tonight, leaving the transmitter and tracking device behind.

Fifteen minutes later she parked in a crowded lot

next to a downtown jazz club called the Blue Parrot. Simon recognized the place. It had been around awhile; he'd been there a few times in his former life in Atlanta. Considering that Jolie hadn't been out other than to dinner in the past three weeks, he wondered why she'd suddenly opted to do so tonight. The call, he reasoned. Someone had invited her there. A stab of jealously seared his gut and he cursed himself for allowing the emotion. Again, he acknowledged how deeply she affected him. Permitting that kind of connection was more than simply against the rules, it was extraordinarily stupid.

Simon stayed in the shadows as he entered the congested night spot. A hulk of a bouncer stationed at the door scanned IDs as patrons breezed by. Simon made no move to offer his and the hulk appeared not to care. A haze of smoke lingered above the throng of tables scattered across the room. A bright spotlight distinguished the stage from the rest of the room and illuminated the band playing there. Couples wrapped in each other's arms swayed to the blues pouring from the brass instruments. Neon lights embellished the jam-packed bar that ran the length of the room to the right of the entrance.

Jolie scooted onto the one unoccupied stool on the far end of the bar. Simon took a position near the corridor leading to the rest rooms and the bank of pay phones across the way, so that he could watch her every move. The hazy shadows would provide adequate cover for him.

He observed those around her for any sign of covert communication, but eventually his gaze shifted back to rest solely on her. She'd ordered a martini and sipped it as if she were completely relaxed, but she was anything but that. She scanned the crowd constantly, her posture rigid. More than once he'd seen her hands shake. To his utter disgust, he noticed a great deal more than those pertinent details. Like the little black dress she wore. It was short and tight, emphasized by high heels that added length to her already incredible legs. The sleeveless sheath plunged low at the throat, and that, too, was accented by the way she wore her hair swept up from her neck, leaving all that creamy smooth terrain completely visible, vulnerable. He licked his lips, hungry at even the idea of tasting her there.

Furious with the path his thoughts insisted upon taking, he gritted his teeth and focused on the truth about Jolie Randolph: she was involved with Raymond Brasco...one way or another. Brasco had killed Simon's partner. Permitting inappropriate thoughts of her was like taking up allegiance with the enemy. The heat in his body subsided just a bit, but not nearly enough.

Forcing himself to study her from a rational perspective, Simon decided she was definitely looking or waiting for someone. He considered the call she had gotten and realized someone was to meet her here. If he was lucky, it would be a definite connection to Brasco, which would make his job a lot easier. And her a lot unluckier.

Maintaining the calm he'd barely achieved grew exceedingly difficult as he watched one guy after another approach her. She shook her head, sending each away with a tremulous smile. Whether they'd offered to buy her a drink or wanted to dance, Simon couldn't be certain, but his relief at her response was undeniable. The thought of some stranger putting his arms around her disturbed him beyond reason.

The next guy proved considerably more persistent. A simple smile and shake of her head didn't send him on his way. Simon's tension ratcheted up another notch at her continued attempts to ward off the jerk's advances. When the guy manacled her arm and moved in too close, Simon was halfway across the smoke filled room before he realized he'd moved.

Fury pounded through him as he pushed through the crowd and moved in next to her, giving the guy holding her arm a look that immediately wilted his arrogant advance.

"Sorry, man," the guy mumbled apologetically after one glimpse of Simon's murderous glare. "I didn't know she was taken."

Jolie's startled gaze collided with Simon's and he wanted to kick himself for revealing his presence. But it was too late now.

"What're you doing—"

"Let's dance," he demanded before she could finish her question. Confusion drew a line between her green eyes. Before she could protest further, he tugged her from the stool and onto the dance floor. By the time he put his arms around her waist and drew her near her confusion had evolved into outright anger.

"You followed me!" she gasped, the words barely distinguishable above the wanton cries of the saxophone.

He shrugged, careful to keep his attention fixed on the fury playing across her lovely face rather than the feel of her slender body in his arms. "You don't believe in coincidences?'' he suggested, leaning closer as he spoke.

Another little gasp drew his gaze to her mouth. Though he didn't hear the sound, he saw the parting of her lips, felt the abrupt rise of her breasts. She countered by flattening her palms against his chest and pushing with all her might.

''I know what you're up to, Simon Ruhl,'' she said furiously, trying again to put some distance between them by shoving him away. She glanced around as if fearful someone would notice the heated exchange. ''I—''

Her gaze abruptly riveted to something beyond his left shoulder and her eyes widened in disbelief or fear. He followed her gaze just in time to see a man with short dark hair turn away and disappear through an emergency exit leading to an alleyway that connected this club with another. Patrons often club-hopped via the alley doors. It wasn't legal, since the exits were clearly marked for emergency use only, but that didn't stop those with enough attitude or alcohol in their systems.

Simon turned back to the woman in his arms and jerked his head toward the exit. ''You know the guy who just left? Did I step in at a bad time?''

She shook her head adamantly, her eyes still wide with apprehension or something of that order. ''I have to go,'' she blurted out. The pulse at the base of her throat fluttered wildly, in perfect time with the rapid rise and fall of her chest. Whoever the guy was he'd scared the hell out of her.

''Let me take you home,'' Simon suggested, uncertain whether he wanted to let her out of his sight even for a split second under current circumstances. Something was definitely wrong here.

Her head moved back and forth again in reply to his offer and she attempted to pull free of his hold, the movement only making him more aware of her soft body.

"Please, I have to go."

Whether it was the ambience, heavy with the despondent sigh of the sax as it hit its final note, or the tears shimmering in her eyes, Simon couldn't say, but he wouldn't let her go like this.

"Jolie, let me drive you home," he coaxed, leaning nearer to ensure she heard his softly uttered words. "You're safe with me."

For one long beat he was certain she would refuse, but then, to his surprise, she nodded in agreement.

Once they were outside he surveyed the parking lot for the dark-haired man. Though he hadn't gotten a good look at his face, Simon had noted his clothing. Red shirt, black trousers. He shouldn't be difficult to spot. But a second visual sweep of the area turned up nothing.

"Did you drive?" he asked, his voice sounding oddly loud in the night despite the applause for the band still shaking the building they'd just exited. The question was unnecessary other than for keeping up the pretense that their running into each other was happenstance.

She nodded. "I parked over there." She pointed to the far side of the parking area, where she'd left her car about an hour prior.

"We'll take your car. I can catch a cab back for mine."

She stole a furtive look from right to left. "I'm

fine, really,'' she insisted, her courage obviously returning. ''I can drive myself home.''

She was probably right. She hadn't finished the one drink she'd ordered, but her blood-alcohol level wasn't his concern at the moment. It was the guy in the red shirt. Simon glanced around once more while she fidgeted with her purse, looking for keys in a bag scarcely large enough to hold a set, much less make locating them difficult. Whoever the guy was he'd done a hell of a job of shaking her up.

When she finally withdrew her keys Simon closed a hand over hers. ''I'd feel better if you let me take you home.'' She started to protest, but he added, ''Please.'' He searched her eyes with his own and said the one thing he thought would sway her stance. ''I think I owe you an apology.''

JOLIE SAT IN THE passenger seat of her car and looked straight ahead. She couldn't look at the man behind the wheel, if she did she might just lose control completely and do something utterly humiliating, like cry. He'd rescued her from that macho jerk who'd tried to force her to dance with him and she'd repaid her gallant rescuer by accusing him of following her. She closed her eyes and sighed softly. God, he must think she was completely nuts.

Then, when he'd kindly offered to drive her home, she'd thrown the gesture in his face.

She was so damned confused. She'd seen the man in the red shirt. The one who'd called. She was certain it was him. He'd looked straight at her and somehow she'd known. There hadn't been a single thing she could put her finger on that she recognized about him and yet she knew him. She was certain of it. He was the one who'd called. He was the one she'd slept with that night…the night she couldn't remember.

Resting her head against the cool glass, she opened her eyes and stared out into the night beyond the headlights cutting a path along the deserted street. She should have followed the guy. All she'd had to do was get away from Simon and she could have had some answers tonight.

Fear tightened the knot in her tummy. What was she thinking? She couldn't just follow some stranger outside! She had no clue who or what he was. He could be a criminal, for all she knew.

But now she might never know.

The way it stood, if she really looked at the situation objectively, *she* was a criminal.

Anxiety and confusion gnawed at her insides. Maybe going to that club had been a mistake. What if the guy took her acceptance of his invitation as his cue to take the next step and come to her house? He knew her phone number. He might just as well know her address.

A new kind of fear rocketed inside her. What if he was following them right now? She twisted around in the seat and peered out the rear window.

"No one is following us," Simon informed her in that deep, reassuring voice that had the power to make her shiver with awareness even now when she was scared to death.

What could she say in response to that statement? That she hadn't thought anyone was following them? Then why had she turned around? Considering her options, she chose to remain silent. Instead, she let the question and worries continue to eat at her. She realized she was wringing her hands, and quickly folded her arms over her chest and tucked her hands safely out of reach of each other. She had to keep it together. Simon couldn't know how close she was to breaking down. She glanced at him. He would put it in his report and then everyone would know that she was losing it. Until that moment she'd forgotten all about the apology he'd used to bait her into this situation. She closed her eyes again and forced away the tumultuous thoughts. None of this made sense. Her whole life was out of control.

When he'd parked the car in her drive, she bounded out before he could open his door. She practically ran up the walk as well as the stairs inside. All she had to do was say good-night at the door and he'd leave. She no longer cared about an apology. She just needed to be alone.

"Thank you," she said when he'd unlocked her door and offered her keys back to her. She manufactured a smile. "I'll see you at the bank on Monday, I suppose."

She tried not to look directly into his eyes. She really did. But it was no use. Though the hall lighting was dim, it didn't diminish the concern she saw in his dark eyes.

"Jolie, let me help you," he urged softly. "All you have to do is trust me."

Terror stabbed her heart and she suddenly wanted desperately to confide in him. He'd encouraged her to do just that all week long, at every opportunity. But she couldn't. She stifled the sob that rose in her throat and grabbed on to her defenses before responding. "I don't know what you mean," she insisted, her voice so shaky he couldn't possibly believe her. "I'm fine. Really. Thank you for driving me home. I think,'' she added, rambling on in spite of the quavery tone she couldn't quite shake, ''that something I ate earlier didn't agree with me.'' She prayed he would accept that explanation of her strange behavior and be on his way.

One second turned to five before he spoke. ''I've pushed you hard all week. I apologize for that, but it's my job. I certainly hope you'll feel better in the morning.'' He smiled, and something deep inside her shifted, made her want to lean against that broad chest and tell him everything. To trust him as he'd insisted she could. ''Good night, Jolie.''

She nodded jerkily. Emotion held her silent. She could only stare into those understanding eyes and wish her secrets weren't so horrible. Then maybe, just maybe, she could confide in him. But she couldn't. He was the enemy, she reminded herself. He was out to get the dirt on her, whatever it might be. *It was his job.* That reminder did nothing to alleviate her vulnerability at the moment. She needed someone right now.

But it couldn't be Simon.

She sucked in an uneven breath. ''Good night.''

Before she could turn away, he moved closer still—so close she could feel his warm breath on her skin. Like an epiphany, the realization that she had subconsciously prayed for this moment since the first time he'd kissed her dawned at that exact instant, and she knew her internal battle was lost. Those full lips brushed her cheek in the barest, sweetest of kisses. ''Pleasant dreams,'' he murmured.

And then he was gone.

Chapter Seven

Saturday brought both relief and a new kind of tension.

Jolie felt incredibly relieved that she didn't have to face Simon Ruhl or the office today. Yet being alone all day in her apartment gave her entirely too much time to think...to replay every moment of the insanity that had started with waking up in the bed of a stranger nearly one week ago.

She shuddered at the thought. She needed someone to talk to. Instantly Simon's voice echoed through her mind. He had urged her to talk to him all week. Insisted that he could help, that he was very good at solving problems. For one beat she considered digging through her purse until she found his card and calling him...and then confessing all.

A stillness claimed her. If she did that, everything she had worked for would be lost. Simon had a job to do—to determine if the bank's employees were trustworthy as well as proficient. Her confession would be an admission to wrongdoing as well as mental instability. Even without the wrongdoing, she would be a liability to the bank. Severe mental illness did not look good on a résumé. Blackouts and illicit behavior were less than desirable, as well.

Jolie recalled her friend Erica's suggestion that perhaps she had been drugged, and grasped the glimmer of solace that accompanied the concept. She could have been drugged. That would explain the blackout. She frowned thoughtfully. But what about the trip to the island, and the bank account? She supposed drugs could somehow explain those anomalies as well, though a significant amount of doubt surrounded that theory.

The dark-haired man she had noticed at the club last night zoomed into her mind's eye. She was very nearly certain it was the same man who'd called her on several occasions this week. He had looked directly at her and there had definitely been something in his eyes—a knowing or understanding. An intimacy, almost. She shivered again and wanted to deny the feeling. But it was true. He knew her somehow.

He could be the key.

She couldn't just sit around waiting for it to happen again. She had to do something. Writing her every move in her journal simply wasn't enough.

But how would she find him?

A new determination in her step, she hurried to the answering machine and checked the caller ID. The number was blocked, so that didn't help. She huffed a disgusted sigh. She could go back to the club tonight. But that was hours away. She needed to do something sooner. Now!

The restaurant! She and Erica had gone to Carlisle's that Sunday night—the night she'd spent with a stranger. She glanced at the wall clock: 5:30 p.m. If she showered and changed now, she could make a seven o'clock reservation. Hang out until nine and then go to the club if he didn't show at the restaurant. It was Saturday night. If he was the partying type he would definitely be at the club tonight.

Anticipation raced through Jolie as she shuffled through her closet in search of something appropriate to wear. She didn't go out often, so her wardrobe was a little lacking in the evening-wear department. Locating a red cocktail dress she'd purchased last year for the bank's annual investors gala, she surveyed it for suitability. Working hard for her next promotion, she had selected the color not only because she looked damn good in it, but for the statement of power it made. Truth was, it had been an impulse buy, one that didn't fit her usually conservative style. She remembered clearly that Mark Boyer had appeared that night wearing a red bow tie with his black tux. He'd been surprised that she would stoop to such tactics of wowing management. Then they'd shared a secret laugh over their matching goals.

The smile that came instantly with that last thought slipped now as she wondered how it was they'd lost even that closeness. The casual friendship they'd once shared had not been cluttered with animosity and professional jealousy. Jolie liked to believe that had Mark gotten the promotion, she would not have turned on him as he had on her. There was a chance, she supposed, that she might have felt exactly the same way had things gone that route.

But they hadn't. She withdrew the dress and the matching high heels from her closet and laid them on the bed. She realized then that Simon wasn't the only person she had to fear. If Mark got an inkling of what was going on, he'd ruin her at the bank. Another shudder quaked through her at the idea that he would like nothing better.

She had to protect herself.

But to do it properly she needed help.

Jolie perched on the edge of the bed and dialed Erica's number. What Jolie needed was Erica watching from a distance. Then if she had another blackout, there would be a witness to exactly what took place. Jolie shook her head. A written journal just wasn't enough. She needed someone watching her when she went out. Someone she could trust.

Erica's answering machine picked up. Jolie hissed a curse as it played her friend's greeting. Unlike Jolie, Erica had a very busy social life. When the woman wasn't out of town, she was out on the town—every night. It amazed Jolie that she had the energy to hold down a full-time, demanding job in corporate advertising while regularly hitting the club scene.

Erica would insist that it was a trade secret and grin like the Cheshire cat.

''Erica, it's Jolie,'' she said, leaving a message in hopes that her friend would get back to her if she wasn't already out on a date. ''If you get this message and don't already have plans, meet me at Carlisle's. I have a seven o'clock reservation. I need to talk.'' The last was said more solemnly than Jolie had intended.

If her friend got the message, she would call. Erica was the one person she could count on in this. Though Jolie loved her father dearly and he would certainly do anything for her, he didn't want to talk about it. She could easily imagine that, since he'd been through it already with her mother, he refused to see it coming again. Denial was no stranger to her, either.

Jolie couldn't blame her father for his self-preserving instincts. He was only human. She wished she didn't see doom coming...but she did.

Sleeping with a stranger, embezzling funds, taking trips she didn't remember—it was all far too familiar. Her mother had made similar mistakes. Eerily similar. Finally, unable to cope with the insanity, she had taken her own life.

Even now Jolie winced at the memory. She had been the one to come home from school and find her mom on the kitchen floor. There had been so much blood—everywhere she had turned. Her mother's lifeless body had been sprawled on the floor, the kitchen knife protruding from her.

Jolie swallowed and forced the images away. There had been much speculation as to why her mother had chosen such a brutal means to end her life. Pills or even a well-placed bullet would have been simpler. Jolie had long ago decided that her mother hadn't planned the act. There had been no suicide note. It was Jolie's firm belief that she had simply reached for the knife in the middle of preparing dinner and done the deed. Perhaps she'd felt the demons that haunted her regaining control once more, and just couldn't bear to go through another episode. Friends and neighbors had talked for months about what a waste her death had been. They couldn't understand how her mother could take her own life, leaving behind a young daughter. How could anyone reach that point?

Jolie dropped down onto the closed toilet seat. Was that where she was headed? She'd only suffered with the uncertainty and blackouts for one week. Fear twisted in her belly. How desperate would she be after an entire year? Who knew how long her mother's problems had been going on before she could no longer hide them? No one. Not even her father knew all that had happened. For months after her mother's death they had discovered purchases and day trips she had made. But the numerous affairs were the worse.

What else had Jolie done that she didn't remember?

Forcing the disturbing thoughts from her mind, she took a long, hot shower, lathering and scrubbing her body as if somehow she could erase the truth. But the reality of the situation wouldn't go away.

No matter how much she wanted for things to go back to the way they had been one week ago, when she'd thought her biggest problem was her deteriorating relationship with her longtime co-worker, Mark, it wasn't to be. For her entire adult life she had been a take-charge woman. She never waited for things to happen or come her way. Jolie Randolph *made* things happen. She sought out the next step. Her new dilemma would be no different. She squared her shoulders and firmed her resolve. It was time for her to investigate the situation further and take charge. She refused to wait for the next episode in the crash-and-burn course destiny appeared to have in store for her.

She would not let this happen.

JUST OVER ONE HOUR LATER she was dressed and ready to go. She'd dried and styled her hair and reapplied her makeup. The red dress and matching high heels accentuated her slender figure. She did, she had to admit, look pretty darned good in the slinky sheath. She surveyed her reflection in the full-length mirror once more. Maybe she had ignored her personal needs for companionship for too long.

The thought instantly conjured the image of Simon Ruhl and his chaste but sizzling kisses. She shivered, but the feeling was pleasurable this time. It contained no fear or uncertainty. She was attracted to the man. And with good reason. He was incredibly handsome. The strength he radiated only made him more desirable. When she had her act together maybe she'd take him up on the offer to get better acquainted that he silently transmitted.

Smiling, the sensation making her step as well as her heart lighter, Jolie locked the front door, floated down the stairs and then strolled toward her car, truly relaxed for the first time all week.

The telephone rang inside her apartment, but she didn't hear it. The answering machine recorded the deep, male voice as it resonated within the protective walls she called home.

"Jolie...I'm waiting for you."

"THIS IS BULL and you know it," Simon roared, his patience at an end.

Cliff Medford wasn't even in the room—or the state, for that matter—and still he'd managed to grind Simon's investigation to a dead stop.

Special Agent Scott Johnson—field supervisor from the Atlanta Bureau office, and the agent in charge of the ongoing case against Raymond Brasco—didn't immediately respond to Simon's summation. Instead, he sat behind his desk and visibly struggled to maintain his calm exterior.

Simon knew the drill. Beneath the customary blue suit beat the heart of a lion who wanted loose from his cage…who wanted to go out and stalk down the bad guys. Johnson was no different from Simon in that respect. The problem was, Johnson was limited by the very Bureau that gave him the jurisdiction to fight crime. He played by the rules and followed the letter of the law. The fact that one of his superiors had given the board of directors of Atlanta's First International Bank a heads-up on their possible connection to this investigation irked Johnson. However, he and Simon were friends, and he had looked the other way, even provided details to Simon as long as passing along the information didn't conflict with the *rules*. The same rules that Simon lived by. But at moments like this those rules seemed a hindrance more than anything else.

"That may very well be," Johnson eventually said. "But Cliff is threatening to go all the way to the top if your involvement on the fringes of this case continues."

Simon gritted his teeth for a moment, forcing himself to take a deep breath. The bastard. "He isn't even involved in this case. You know what the problem is." Simon paused to regain some semblance of composure. "It's been four years. If I can get past it, surely he can." After all, it wasn't Medford's mistake that had gotten Simon's partner killed. It was his own. Now was his opportunity to make the man responsible pay. He wanted that opportunity. No one—not Medford, not Jolie Randolph—would take it from him.

"That's the problem," Johnson stated. "Cliff is insisting to my boss that your involvement in this case will jeopardize everything we've worked months to accomplish. He cites your record with Brasco as his foundation for the insinuation." He eyed Simon speculatively. "I'm certain you would tell me if there was any truth to his accusation."

Simon didn't have time for this. He should be watching Jolie right now. She was extremely vulnerable. He felt certain he was on the verge of discovering something very important. He'd gotten only a glimpse of the guy making eye contact with her last night, but his instincts had gone on point. His gut told him that the man was the connection he needed. Simon had been in this business too long to be very far off the mark, personal involvement or not. He was close and he knew it.

He looked straight into his old friend's eyes and told him the truth. "If I denied some amount of personal motive, I'd be lying. Raymond Brasco killed my partner—you know that. If I can help bring him down, I will. But I won't jeopardize my case or the Bureau's to accomplish that end. You know me better than that."

Not even breathing, he waited for Johnson to make his decision. Simon kept his tone and his expression carefully devoid of the anger and desire for revenge raging inside him. He'd never be able to do this without the Bureau's assistance. So far he'd only allowed any real emotion to show when he'd complained about Medford. That was to be expected. He still had this game under control. And that's all it was. Medford had turned it into one. He held a grudge against Simon. He'd only gotten the promotion four years ago because Simon declined the position. Medford hadn't gotten over that blow to his enormous ego yet. Simon doubted he ever would. The relocation to the Birmingham office hadn't helped.

"You're right," Johnson admitted with a relieved

sigh. "I do know you better than that. You'll bow out before you'll jeopardize the case." He stood and reached for his jacket, which hung on a slender oak rack in the corner near his credenza. "I promised the wife I'd take her out to dinner tonight. It's our anniversary." He flashed Simon a smile and patted his pocket. "Thankfully, I didn't forget the gift, but I should get going or even an anniversary ring won't get me out of hot water for being so late."

Simon glanced at his watch. It was nearly 8:00 p.m. already. Damn. He'd left surveillance of Jolie's apartment more than an hour ago. He hadn't had the opportunity to put a tracking device in her car. He mentally rolled his eyes. Who was he kidding? He'd had the opportunity, he'd just fallen down on the job, too overwhelmed by forbidden emotions to think straight. The one he'd put in her purse had gotten shoved into a drawer somewhere in her apartment. He had to get back to Jolie now. Every minute was crucial. He pushed himself to his feet and extended his hand to his old friend. "I appreciate your understanding in the matter."

Johnson pumped his hand once, then studied him a moment. "I know how much you want to see Brasco go down for what he's done, and I do trust your judgment, Simon. But I had to be sure." He looked directly at Simon. "I had to look you in the eye and hear it in your own words."

Simon nodded and followed him from the office.

Guilt weighed heavily on his shoulders. He tried to shake it off, but it wasn't budging. Everything he'd said was true. He would never intentionally interfere with the proper procedures and conduction of an investigation. Still, he did have a hidden agenda. He intended to make the connection to Brasco for money laundering, and he intended to bring him down no matter the cost.

For keeping that to himself, he couldn't dismiss the guilt.

Before leaving him he wished his old friend a happy anniversary. Once in his SUV, Simon wondered why the idea of Johnson's anniversary and the wife waiting at home suddenly made him feel regret. He'd noticed the framed photographs stationed on his desk. There was a baby, too. Johnson definitely appeared to have it all. His career, a family.

Simon had never really considered having it all.

Right now he wanted only one thing—to bring down Raymond Brasco.

JOLIE SAT ALONE at a table for two in a discreet corner of Carlisle's. The ambience was very romantic. The lights were low and the music soft. The occasional clink of crystal or rap of silver against china was the only interruption to the quiet elegance.

She looked at her gold wristwatch, the one her father had given her for graduation a decade ago, and realized it was almost eight already.

And she was still alone.

He wasn't going to show.

She sighed and sipped her white wine to occupy her hands. She didn't know his name. How on earth did she expect to find him? Just because she thought their connection had begun in this restaurant meant nothing. She could be wrong. He might not even be the stranger with whom she'd spent that lost night. He could be more trouble.

Uneasiness slid through her at that last possibility.

She didn't need more trouble. Her heart fluttered with the new stress. She didn't need more stress, either. To bolster her courage she drained her glass. She'd never been much of a drinker, enjoying the occasional glass of wine, nothing more. She prayed now that the smooth, fruity liquid would calm the tremor in her hands and the screaming fear in her brain.

Nausea roiled and she was suddenly certain she was going to be sick. "Oh, no." She jumped up from the table so quickly her wineglass bumped against her water goblet. Those seated around her stopped to stare. Suddenly unable to breathe, Jolie rushed to the ladies' room.

Not until the door closed like a safety barrier behind her was she able to take a breath. She sagged against the wall and fought to draw more air into her lungs and at the same time bring her heart rate back down to normal. She couldn't do this if she didn't stay in complete control. If he showed now, she'd be in no condition to do what had to be done. She had to listen, to observe. Running into him someplace like this might be her only chance to find the truth.

Taking her time, she gulped several more deep breaths and released them slowly. Once the spinning in her head had stopped, and her stomach had ceased to churn so violently, she pushed off from the wall and crossed the comfortable sitting room to the more functional area beyond. She moistened a towel with cool water and dabbed at her throat. Lifting her hair, she did the same to the back of her neck. When she felt reasonably calm again she checked her appearance and headed back out to wait for the man who knew the truth she so desperately needed.

She chastised herself for running scared. Nerves.

Her stomach was upset because she was nervous. Getting a firmer grip on her composure would settle things down. She needed answers. Answers only *he* could give. If only he would show. And if he did, the last thing she wanted to do was scare him off.

He was there.

She drew up short, the air stalling in her lungs.

He'd looked directly at her last night at the club. She would never forget the intimate knowledge in his eyes. He knew things about her she needed to know. And now he was here. She wasn't dreaming or imagining anything. He sat at her table, waiting patiently, as if he'd known she would return at any moment.

Renewed anxiety curled through her. The need to run kicked her heart back into overdrive. But she had to think. Had to figure out what to do next. She knew nothing about this man. He could be a serial killer for all she knew. A rapist. She shuddered. But he was the only link she had between sanity and the nightmare of not knowing.

She needed him.

Catching sight of her, he stood and smiled invitingly. "I see you chose our favorite table."

Jolie gasped at the timbre of the voice she'd been waiting all evening to hear. The sound escaped her lips before she could stop it. It was definitely him. He loomed over her table, as tall and powerfully frightening as she remembered from last night. Finally, when her lungs could bear the pressure no longer, she released a pent-up breath and summoned a reply.

"I didn't know if you'd come." She scarcely recognized the thin, shaky voice as her own.

"You knew I'd come," he insisted in that mysterious tone that spoke of intimacy—the one that frightened her the most. He moved to the chair she'd vacated so hastily and waited for her to take her seat. "I don't know why you play these games with me, Jolie. You know how crazy it makes me."

She swallowed with difficulty and searched for the right response. Instead, she sat down and allowed him to push her chair in for her. The feel of his fingers against her bare arms made her tremble. How could she do this? Her heart threatened to burst from her chest and her head was spinning again. Seemingly oblivious to her plight, he settled in the chair directly across from her and summoned the waiter.

While she waged war with the fear mounting inside her, he ordered her another white wine and a Scotch for himself. Then he reached across the table and took her hand. She resisted the urge to draw away, though she could do nothing about the added quaking his touch elicited. She had to let this play out. Had to be strong. She needed answers.

"There is no need for these games, Jolie," he persisted, as if they had known each other for ages. "It isn't necessary for you to try and intrigue me." He squeezed her hand affectionately. "I'm already very much intrigued."

Dear God, who was this man? As he leaned forward to kiss the hand he held so firmly in his own, Jolie struggled not to flinch, and at the same time worked up the courage to ask the question burning in her throat. "Who...who are you?"

A smile widened his lips as they grazed her knuckles. She suppressed another tremble. She had to do this. Had to keep her cool. Had to play along. Please, please, just let him tell her the truth.

He straightened, still clutching her hand, his gaze

leveled on hers. "More games?" He laughed softly. "In that case, I'll be whoever you want me to be."

The way he caressed her hand, the insistent urging of his voice…it was all so alien and yet so keenly familiar. Her head spun again with the effort to recall that lost night. To remember any other moment she had spent with the man. Just then the waiter arrived to freshen their drinks.

"So." The man drank deeply from his glass, then licked the residue from his lips. "What game are we playing tonight?"

Jolie had never played games, sexual or otherwise. She had no idea what he meant. But she had to fake it. She had to keep him talking. "Why don't you choose?" she suggested, then reached for her wine. Abruptly she remembered the possibility of it being drugged, and snatched back her hand. Though she'd seen the waiter pour the wine, she wouldn't risk it. This man, the stranger she'd come here to find, could have put something in her glass while she was in the powder room. Her head was already spinning and her stomach still churning. Besides, she needed to keep her mind as clear as possible. She'd already had one glass of wine for courage. She couldn't risk any more.

His smile widened and his expression turned blatantly sexual. "It would be my pleasure," he said in answer to her suggestion.

His image blurred. Jolie blinked repeatedly and peered at him. Looking into those eyes, seeing the infinite satisfaction her uneasiness gave him was the last thing Jolie would remember that night.

A WHISPER TICKLED her ear, but she refused to move or to even acknowledge it.

She didn't want to wake up, except something nudged at her, urged her to do so. It was almost as if a little voice cried, *Wake up! Wake up!* But she was only dreaming. It couldn't be anything else. It was Sunday morning. She always slept in on Sunday morning. Well, sometimes she went to church. But she hadn't in a very long time. Maybe she should. It would be good for her soul.

Rousing slightly, Jolie felt the silky whisper against her skin once more. She cracked her eyes open just a fraction. A large ceiling fan rotated overhead, stirring the silence, creating a soft breeze. Her eyes slid closed once more as she made a sound of contentment. She'd meant to get a ceiling fan in her bedroom. She'd had one back home growing up. But there never seemed to be time to get anything done around her apartment.

Something negative crept into her thoughts, and she frowned. If she didn't have a ceiling fan…why was one circling overhead? She opened her eyes once more, a little wider this time. The fan was there, turning slowly. The blades were a glossy white embellished with gold trim, going round and round and round. She squeezed her eyes shut once more, and her stomach contracted savagely. Moments later, when she could bear to open her eyes again, she forced herself to turn to the right and look there. The movement sent a spear of pain shattering through her skull. A moan echoed. She was pretty sure it came from her.

It took some time, but eventually details registered. Furniture…clothes scattered about haphazardly. The room was dimly lit. Beyond the foot of the bed was a shuttered window, but the sun leaking in through the slats told her it was daytime.

Where was she?

A memory of waking up in another strange room slashed through her brain. A scream caught in her throat. Her body went rigid as ice slid through her veins.

Where was she?

She looked to her right again.

Nothing she saw was even vaguely familiar.

This wasn't the same bedroom as last time. Not nearly so elegant. She remembered that much.

Then where was she?

Snippets of sitting alone in the restaurant flickered through her mind. Then more images, this time including a dark-haired man. Not Simon Ruhl. Someone else.

The man.

The voice on the telephone.

Jolie sat up, her breath catching with the fear that soared inside her.

She'd done it again.

Her gaze dropped to her chest, where she instinctively held the sheet over her bare breasts.

Her heart pounding, she stumbled from the bed, dragging the sheet with her.

She swiped the hair from her face, only then realizing that she was crying. What had she done? A glimpse of crimson flashed at the edge of her vision. The dress. She'd worn that red dress last night. She blinked and looked again. But it wasn't the dress...it was the corner of the sheet.

Blood.

The heart that hammered in her chest suddenly stalled.

Was she bleeding?

She lifted the sheet from her naked body and stared down at herself. Nothing…no wounds, no blood.

But where had the blood come from?

She lifted her gaze upward…to the bed.

A scream burgeoned in her throat.

The man who'd met her at the restaurant last night was there—in the bed. A large kitchen knife protruded from his chest. There was blood…*everywhere*.

And she suddenly knew exactly what had happened.

She'd killed him.

Dear God, she'd killed a man.

Help.

She needed help.

The police.

Fear roared inside her head, the only part of her that wasn't numb. She couldn't call the police.

Simon…she could call Simon.

Chapter Eight

Simon stood in the bedroom doorway and surveyed the grim scene before moving into the room. The victim was male, his nude body sprawled on the rumpled bed linens, a large kitchen knife protruding from his chest. Jolie cowered behind Simon, a bloodstained bed sheet twisted around her. He didn't have to ask to know that she was nude, as well.

She'd called his cell phone, hysterical and crying that she needed his help. When he'd asked where she was she'd had to search the place for the address. She'd had no idea. Then, when he'd arrived, she'd frantically described waking up to this scene. Immediately after recounting the chilling moments she'd fallen silent, defensively retreating into herself.

"Stay here," he said to her, noting the glassy-eyed gaze staring back at him. Shock was a definite concern here. "Maybe you should lie down on the sofa."

She glanced at the sofa and shook her head, the movement strained, unnatural. "No. I'll stay right here." She sagged against the wall next to the bedroom door. She shook her head again and muttered, "I can't...."

"All right." He brutally shoved all emotion aside

and forced himself to see the scene from a profiler's perspective. Clothes were strewn about, male as well as female items. His gaze veered back to the red dress lying amid the chaos, and his mind instantly provided an image of Jolie wearing the sensual garment. He blinked the picture away, but not before it had its effect. His body hardened with equal parts fury and jealousy that she'd worn the dress for another man. He clenched his jaw so tightly a muscle there started to tick as he refocused on the crime scene.

Nothing else about the room appeared to be disturbed. The decorating in the bedroom, like the rest of the apartment, was austere, the furnishings elaborate yet contemporary. The location spoke of wealth. Simon didn't have to take a closer look at the male clothing to know designer labels would be present. He crossed the thickly carpeted floor to the discarded trousers and removed the wallet from the back pocket. He opened it and searched until he discovered the driver's license.

Ice formed in his gut when he read the name boldly printed next to the unbecoming snapshot of a man in his late twenties. Simon swore softly and hoped against hope that it was a mistake. Careful of any evidence in his path, he moved to the bedside and compared the picture on the license to the ashen face of the victim. The eyes were open wide, a permanent expression of astonishment stiffened into his features.

It was him.

Simon swore again.

The telephone on the bedside table drew his attention and he reached for it. He hesitated as the events to come flashed in rapid succession through his mind. The police would arrive in mere minutes. Crime

Scene Investigation would follow. Jolie would be taken in for questioning, then arrested when her fingerprints were lifted from the murder weapon.

It was all too easy.

Why the hell hadn't he blown off Johnson last night and kept up his surveillance? Why hadn't he kept his head on straight where she was concerned? He could have prevented this tragedy. Gritting his teeth against the emotions bombarding him, Simon surveyed the bed once more. The victim's hands were clenched into fists. There was no other sign of a struggle. Simon turned on the bedside lamp. He'd already flipped on the overhead light to survey the room. He crouched next to the bed and studied the victim's hands. He viewed each carefully, inspecting the fingers. A single hair was trapped between the middle and index finger of his right hand.

His investigator's sense screaming at him, Simon ignored the warning and cautiously removed the trapped hair. He held it beneath the lamplight and noted the characteristics: black, much shorter than Jolie's blond tresses, yet too long to be the victim's despite the similarity in coloring. And the victim's was more brown than black. The sense of relief that surged through Simon made him weak.

Cursing himself for behaving so foolishly, Simon placed the hair exactly as he'd found it, then stood. This had to be a setup. He could feel it. Of course, it would take a lot more than a single unidentified hair to pin the murder on someone other than Jolie, who'd awakened in bed next to the victim, but it confirmed what Simon's instincts told him. Jolie was a pawn in some sort of plan. Whatever was to ultimately happen, the orchestrator would get away clean and Jolie

would take the fall. But what the hell were they after?
He stared down at the dead man. And how did this
murder play into it? Was there someone new attempting to take over the local mob empire?

Jolie still waited outside the bedroom door as he
moved back through it. She didn't speak, didn't ask
him what he was doing. The urge to comfort her was
nearly overpowering.

But there wasn't time now.

He had to keep his head on straight this time. He
surveyed the apartment once more, going more slowly
this time. Nothing was out of place. Jolie's purse had
been strategically placed under the coffee table so she
probably wouldn't see it if she awoke and rushed out
before the police were summoned. A shoe peeked
from beneath the sofa.

Simon gathered the items, moving through the
apartment until he'd found all that she'd likely worn.
Red silk panties and bra, the shoes and purse, and
finally the dress. He struggled to keep his respiration
even as he did what had to be done next. It was
against everything he'd ever learned—against every
professional ethic he'd ever possessed—but he had to
do it. This was wrong and he knew it. She was innocent. He ignored the remote possibility that *he*
could be wrong, that he could be allowing emotion to
rule his thinking.

He examined the bedroom once more, slowly, me-
thodically, and found nothing else belonging to her.
He placed the items in a pile next to her outside the
bedroom door. She remained exactly where he'd left
her, leaning against the wall, her eyes glazed, her
body trembling.

Forcing his attention back to the problem at hand,

Simon next did the one thing that he would once have
sworn he would never do: he wiped the handle of the
knife clean. Aware his efforts were likely futile, he
wiped down the most obvious areas, knowing he'd
never remove all the prints he or she might have left,
only the most damning ones. If, in fact, the real killer
had left any prints there, Simon had just destroyed the
evidence, but it was a chance he'd have to take.

Between the thundering in his chest and the voice
of conscience ranting in his brain, he could scarcely
think. But he could feel, and he couldn't let this go
down this way. He visually examined Jolie once
more. There was no blood on her hands. He tugged
the sheet from her and allowed it to drop to the floor.
Swallowing tightly, he let his gaze continue downward, along creamy smooth skin. He tried to be ob-
jective about what he saw, but no part of him proved
unaffected. She was beautiful. Even with tears stain-
ing her cheeks and fear ravishing her extraordinary
green eyes.

Forcing himself to see beyond all that, he made
certain he couldn't find the first smudge of blood on
her body. Whoever had done this had made two mistakes. He or she had left a single hair that belonged
to neither the victim, who had dark brown hair, nor
the intended suspect, who was blond. And the perp
had failed to see that at least some blood ended up
on the intended suspect. No way could a knife wound
that deep and deadly have been inflicted without
things getting a little messy. Then again, Jolie could
have showered after the act. Simon looked at the sheet
and considered that she might have wiped herself
clean in that way, as well. He checked her hands

again, his movements impatient, rougher than he'd intended, but she didn't resist.

Ignoring for the moment the possibility that she could be a murderess, he tugged the dress over her shoulders, guiding her arms and then raising the zipper. Though she appeared not to care if he covered her or not, he needed her covered. He placed the shoes at her feet but didn't bother urging her to put them on. Instead, he tucked the panties and bra into his jacket pocket and took the sheet back to the bed to attempt to determine how it had become stained. After replacing it, he could easily see that the sheet had been draped over the victim, probably hitting just beneath his waist when the fatal wound was inflicted. The best Simon could estimate, it had remained so, soaking up the pooling blood until Jolie dragged it from the bed to cover herself.

Simon scrubbed a hand over his face and tried to think if he'd covered the bases enough to throw whoever investigated the murder off Jolie's scent. He'd done all he could do. Now he had to get her out of here before anyone saw her. That would be the difficult part. Especially with her in that red dress.

Back in the short hallway that separated the bedroom from the main living area, Simon grasped Jolie's arm and reclaimed her purse.

"We have to go," he told her when she looked at him.

Her eyes were wild with fear as she searched his face, recognition flaring. "We need to do something," she said brokenly. "He—he…"

Simon shook his head. "There's nothing else we can do."

JOLIE SAID NOTHING as Simon drove to the apartment he'd leased for the duration of this assignment. She needed a sedative and some sleep. The former he couldn't do much about, but he could see that she got the latter. He glanced at her when he parked in the basement garage, and chastised himself again for tampering with evidence. For being a complete fool.

It wasn't until he ushered her into his dark apartment that she hesitated.

"Why are we here?" She peered up at him like a frightened bird, her trembling arms draped around her slender body in a protective manner.

"You'll be safe here," he assured her. "You need to sleep."

She seemed to consider his words, then nodded and allowed him to guide her into the bedroom. He tossed her purse aside and found her a shirt to use as a gown. He gestured to the bathroom. "You can change in there."

She nodded again and started forward just as he remembered her underthings. "You might want these," he said, holding out the red silky garments. She accepted the items without really looking at them, and disappeared into the en suite bathroom.

While she changed, Simon drew back the covers and made a decision about how he was going to handle the situation. He was in deep trouble any way he looked at it, but he'd just have to live with that. It was too late now to change what he'd done. He tried to rationalize his actions, but there was no rationale. He'd crossed the line, tampered with evidence, and he still didn't fully understand what had possessed him to do so.

As if to toss the answer in his face, Jolie padded

across the room, her movements stiff and awkward. He tamped down the urge to hold her and tell her everything would be all right. He couldn't make that promise and he knew it, but he wanted to and that was bad enough. That he couldn't resist looking at her with desire in his eyes and need in his gut made him even angrier at himself. Where the hell was his objectivity? His professional common sense? Lost, he admitted. How the hell had this happened?

She slid between the cool sheets and pulled the comforter up to her chin. "Thank you," she murmured, her voice fragile with emotions.

He couldn't respond. He could only stand there and watch her until she drifted off to sleep. He'd screwed up royally this time. He'd tampered with evidence and fallen for the primary suspect. The realization startled him. And all this time he'd considered himself invincible, untouchable. Not even in the Brasco trial had he done anything so incredibly stupid when it came to making the case. The warrant had been handled correctly, he knew. But the judge had ruled against him. In time Simon had realized the judge had been bought and paid for. Simon's one mistake had been in being too cocky—letting his emotions guide him. And here he was, doing the same thing again. This time he had to make sure his error in judgment didn't get anyone killed.

Turning away from the vulnerable and innocent vision Jolie made sleeping like a trusting child, he strode into the living room, cursing himself every step of the way.

He flipped open his cell phone and made the call that could be postponed no longer.

Johnson's gruff voice answered on the second ring.

"There's been a murder," Simon told him flatly. What was the point in prettying it up with a lengthy prologue? Nothing. "You'll likely find my prints there," he added. He considered mentioning the hair he'd found in the victim's right hand, but that sounded too much like staging. Better to let the forensic techs find it on their own.

"What the hell are you talking about, Ruhl?" Johnson was fully awake now.

"Here's the address," Simon continued, ignoring his question. He quickly rattled off the location. "Just keep the heat off me and my case as long as you can. That's all I ask. You can do that for me, can't you, Johnson?"

Johnson owed him. Simon didn't have to remind him of that little detail. When one agent took a bullet for another, it wasn't necessary to do any reminding. That was the reason Johnson had so willingly fed him information on the ongoing case. It was also the reason he'd ignored Medford's ranting. But it had been a long time ago. Up to this point both he and Johnson had avoided the issue.

The sigh on the other end of the line told Simon that it was a done deal. He didn't have to worry for a little while, anyway. Unless the answer to the next question no doubt coming changed all that.

"Who cashed in?" Johnson demanded, as he fished for pen and paper.

Simon swallowed hard, putting off the inevitable for an additional three seconds. This was the part that made the least sense of all. "Ray Brasco, Jr.," he announced. "The old man's only son."

JOLIE'S EYELIDS DRIFTED slowly open. A distant ache accompanied the movement. Her head. She groaned. She felt as if she had a hangover.

The horror of waking up next to a dead man slammed into her brain like the engines of a rocket exploding for liftoff.

She'd killed a man.

No!

She sat up, only then realizing she was in bed.

She couldn't have killed anyone.

She would never harm a soul.

The blood.

The knife.

Just like she'd found her mother.

The whole gruesome scene whirled through the private theater of her mind. First the horror of finding her mother, then the shock of discovering the dead man lying next to her. She shuddered and nausea boiled up in her throat.

Jolie threw the covers back and dashed for the bathroom. When she'd heaved until her entire body hurt, she rinsed her mouth and stared at the reflection in the mirror.

How could she have done such a thing?

How could she not remember?

She frowned, tears burning in her eyes. She remembered sitting in the restaurant. She remembered looking into his eyes. But that was it. She didn't even know his name. She peered down at her trembling hands. How could she have plunged that knife into his chest?

Why would she have done such a thing?

She didn't even know him.

Why couldn't she remember anything? She massaged her aching forehead with the tips of her fingers.

She'd had one glass of wine…that was all. He'd offered her another drink, but she'd declined. What had happened after that?

Where was she now?

Renewed horror exploded inside her.

Simon.

Simon had rescued her.

She was at his place.

Though she really didn't remember how she'd gotten here, it was such a blur, she did know with certainty that he had taken care of her.

"Okay," she ordered the pathetic woman in the mirror, "get a grip. You've got to sort this out. It can't be real," she added. She shook her head and forced the images away. She had to find Simon. To see if he knew what had really happened and who the dead man was. Maybe there wasn't even a dead man. Maybe it was just a nightmare.

She shivered again. Wrapping her arms around herself, she staggered back into the bedroom. She paused a moment to regain her equilibrium. Whatever she'd drank had seriously messed with her head. But that was impossible, wasn't it? It was only wine. She'd watched the waiter pour it.

It didn't make sense. Had she eventually shared a drink with the man? She clearly remembered deciding not to.

The elegant draperies of Simon's bedroom abruptly snagged her attention, and Jolie turned slowly to survey the room. It looked so familiar. But that wasn't possible. She'd never been to Simon's home before. The massive wing chairs stood like sentinels near the heavy, luxurious drapes shading the massive windows. A chill sank deeper inside her as she likened the deep burgundy color to the bloodstained sheets.

Snippets of recognition humming inside, momentarily overriding the stark memory of murder, she moved toward the windows. When she drew the velvety fabric away from the glass, she gasped at the beautiful view of downtown Atlanta. She'd seen this before. She released the drapery and turned around to scan the room once more. The lavish furnishings, the thick carpeting…it was just as she remembered it.

This was the room she'd awakened in on Monday morning.

Uncertainty and confusion punched her in the stomach. How could that be?

Hugging herself even more tightly, she moved soundlessly from the room. Where was Simon? She shivered. This didn't make sense. Why would she have awakened in his bedroom? And why wouldn't he have mentioned it to her at some point this week? He'd pretended that they'd never met.

She hesitated. Maybe this whole thing had been a terrible dream. Maybe it was still Monday and this entire crazy week was just a part of that waking nightmare.

Her pulse jumping with anticipation, she hastened her step, searching for Simon. She found him stretched out on the sofa, his eyes closed in sleep. Her hopes plummeted to her feet when she noticed the red purse lying on the coffee table adjacent to the sofa. She'd worn the red dress. She remembered far too clearly now. Determination had driven her to find answers.

None of it had been a mere dream.

The realization made her knees give way and she sank to the floor next to the sofa.

She'd killed a man.

A man she didn't even know.

Tears brimmed, then rolled down her cheeks.

Her life was over.

She was an embezzler and a murderer. She wasn't like her mother at all. She was far, far worse.

Why had Simon helped her? She stared at the sleeping man who had come to her rescue. He'd hounded her at work all week long and then he'd rescued her from a murder scene.

Question after question spilled one over the other into a jumble. Somehow this wasn't right. She swiped at her cheeks and forced herself to think rationally. Why would he do all this? Why was any of this happening to her? She had to think. To focus and somehow make sense of this insanity. She ordered her fuzzy brain to consider the details, but the man who proved her savior distracted her again.

Simon had changed clothes. He no longer wore the black suit she'd come to associate with his tall, dark and dangerous good looks. The trousers were navy and he wore no shirt. For one second her gaze roved the mesmerizing terrain of sculpted muscle before she realized why he'd changed. The blood. He'd likely gotten blood on his clothes. Or maybe he just felt dirty after touching death...a murder she had committed.

She stared down at him now, her confusion so complete she felt ready to scream with it. Who the hell was he? Why would a bank auditor do such things to protect someone he scarcely knew?

The gun lying on the coffee table just beyond her

purse suddenly drew her attention. She shivered. Why would he carry a weapon? What did a bank auditor need with a gun? His wallet lay there, too. She focused on the wallet, knowing it would contain ID. If she looked at it she would know who he really was, if he wasn't a mere auditor.

With her head thumping so loud she feared it would wake him, she reached for the wallet and quickly found what she needed.

Simon Ruhl didn't even live in Atlanta—at least he hadn't until recently. He was a resident of Chicago, the Illinois license showed. Another card identified him as an investigator for a firm called the Colby Agency. A *private* investigations firm. A new kind of fear chilled her blood.

Why had Mr. Knox introduced him as a member of the audit team?

Everything inside her stilled as the epiphany dawned clearly as day. Because the bank's board of directors or the audit team or maybe both wanted him to look beyond where they had the capability of seeing.

Simon Ruhl was a spy.

The breath rushed out of her lungs in one long whoosh.

A strong hand suddenly snaked out and manacled her wrist before she could place the wallet back on the table. Her gaze flew to Simon's.

"Did you find what you were looking for?" he asked, his voice gruff with sleep or maybe with anger.

"Why are you here?" she demanded, too furious herself to care about his emotional state.

Simon considered lying, but opted for the truth. He released her and sat up. She scrambled away from him, putting the coffee table between them in a defensive maneuver.

"The bank hired me to look into any possible money laundering activities taking place. A friend at the FBI had given the board the heads-up on an investigation they were about to launch. Atlanta's First International Bank had been named as a possible player in the investigation. The head start gave the bank the opportunity to clear up the situation, which the directors were convinced had to be a mistake, before the feds had to step in."

Money laundering? "Have you lost your mind?" Jolie climbed into a chair opposite him. "There's no money laundering going on at my bank," she argued, though he could see her mind whirling with questions and possibilities, one of which made her intensely uneasy.

Despite the fact that during this investigation he'd broken every rule he'd sworn to abide by in order to help her, for just one moment he wondered if he was wrong. Could she be as guilty as someone wanted her to look? Or was she experiencing some sort of emotional breakdown? Simon knew her family history. He'd read all about her mother and the illness that had plagued her. Jolie's behavior at times mimicked the symptoms of the disease, but his gut told him there was more at play here than genetics. Especially considering the other family secret he had uncovered—a secret she didn't even know about. Logic, however, warned him that his emotions were playing a large part in his conclusions.

Simon's unwavering gaze allowed Jolie to see that he knew something she didn't. "You're wrong," he said with finality, confirming her suspicion. "That's exactly what's going on, and you're somehow connected.''

That was ludicrous. He was accusing her of the crime. He didn't have to say that; she could see it in those dark eyes. He suspected her. She shot to her feet and glared down at him. ''That's ridiculous. I don't even know any bad guys. How could I be laundering money for someone?''

That penetrating gaze stared right through her every defense, unnerving her all the more when she was certain things couldn't get any worse. It wasn't just him, she suddenly realized, it was the board of directors. Possibly even Mr. Knox. She remembered her boss's uncharacteristic concern…the questions. God, he knew. Maybe she had done all those things. The image of the dead man, a knife sprouting from his chest and blood everywhere, overpowered her, and she sank back into the chair.

''The dead man was Raymond Brasco, Jr.,'' Simon explained as if reading her mind. ''Sound familiar?''

She frowned, racking her brain for any recognition. Finally she shook her head. ''I don't know the name.'' She looked directly at Simon. ''I know how this all looks.'' She clenched her hands into fists to keep them still. ''But I didn't kill anyone.'' Her voice caught and she had to take a moment to regroup before she added, ''I couldn't do anything like that.''

''If I thought you had, you wouldn't be here right now.''

Relief, so profound that she wanted to weep, gushed through her. He was telling the truth. He wouldn't have helped her unless he'd thought she was innocent. ''I don't know what happened,'' she admitted, her voice small, the terror in her heart echoed there. "I can't remember anything after the restaurant."

"Were you supposed to meet anyone at the restaurant?"

She shook her head. "I went there to see if the man who kept calling me would show. I've been there dozens of times." She and Erica frequented Carlisle's. It was her friend's favorite restaurant. But Jolie didn't bother explaining all that. It didn't make a difference.

"Ray Brasco has been calling you?"

Something had changed in Simon's voice. It scared Jolie. There was something savage in his tone. She forced her head to move up and down in answer to his question. "I don't know why. It all started this week."

He leaned forward and braced his arms on his widespread knees. "Tell me everything. From the beginning."

How could she do that? Then he would know the whole truth. She wilted, the anxiety so thick and heavy it hindered her ability to breathe. But how could she not tell him? He was all that stood between her and a murder charge. She had to trust him. Not giving herself a chance to second-guess her decision, she told him everything from the moment she'd woken up in a strange bed on Monday morning, to the odd call about the foreign account, concluding with last night's rendezvous with the murder victim. She even told him about her mother's illness and how she believed she was falling victim to the same disorder.

Only when she'd finished did she remember that it was Simon's bed in which she'd woken that first

morning. Anger jolted her once more, making a tiny
dent in her other emotions. "Why didn't you tell me
that I spent the night here last Sunday?" Her tone left
no question as to how she felt about his deceit. "The
truth would have saved me a lot of unnecessary
worry."

He studied her a moment before responding. The
idea that that dark gaze had seen all of her made her
skin heat with desire. She silently railed at herself.
Wasn't she in enough trouble now? Did she have to
continue to respond so stupidly?

"When you didn't remember, I decided it was for
the best. I didn't want that standing between us."

Wringing her hands in her lap, she asked the other
question that had to be answered. "Did we…" She
stared straight into those dark eyes. "Did we have
sex?" The idea that she'd had sex with a stranger,
even one as handsome and alluring as Simon, had
haunted her all week.

He shook his head slowly from side to side. "I
helped you into bed. That's all."

Confusion reigned supreme once more. "But I was
naked. You—"

He shook his head. "You undressed yourself. I
tried to stop you, but you insisted."

She looked away, her cheeks burning with humiliation.

"You weren't yourself," he offered, his voice gentle. "I believe now that you'd been drugged."

Her gaze swung back to his. She'd considered that
possibility. "Why do you believe that?" That would
explain so much. She wanted to cling to that hope,
but she couldn't. Not yet.

"When you left the restaurant that night you

walked right into me as if you didn't even see me.'' He shrugged those broad shoulders. ''Passed out right in my arms.''

She threaded her fingers through her hair and struggled to remember the events of that lost night. ''I don't understand how that could have happened.''

''It probably happened just as it did last night. You disappeared on me the next morning before I could explain what had occurred, and suggest that you take a blood test.''

''Wait!'' This was too much. She surged to her feet and paced the floor in front of the coffee table once more. ''Why didn't you just tell me that night at Lebron's when you approached me?''

He was the one to look away this time.

Realization hit her like a sucker punch to the gut. ''Oh, God. It is me,'' she said, the words flowing out in a painful breath. ''The bank thinks I'm the one who's doing the money laundering. They sent you to investigate *me*.''

It all made sense now. She was losing her mind. And along the way she'd started associating with mobsters.

''It's not that simple,'' Simon protested. His words did nothing to assuage her anxiety.

She glared at him, determined to learn the whole truth. ''It is that simple. I'm the suspect. I've admitted to embezzling.'' She flung her arms heavenward. ''I can't even remember doing it, but I obviously did.'' She turned and paced back in the opposite direction. ''It's not much of a stretch to money laundering. Who knows what kind of secret life I could have been living all this time without even remembering?''

Simon couldn't bear the hurt and fear in her eyes

a moment longer. He wanted to tell her she wasn't losing her mind—that she wasn't suffering from the illness that had plagued her mother. "It's not you," he lied outright. He could at least give her that now. "It's Boyer."

Shock radiated through her once more. He watched her slender body tremble with the force of it. She was exhausted and very nearly at the end of her emotional rope. He had to make her believe that she was safe. He needed to make her believe it. He needed her. Unfortunately, that need went well beyond the professional. Damn, he was a fool.

"Mark? That's impossible." She shook her head. "With the blackouts I've been having, I'd suspect me way before him. He wouldn't hurt a fly much less kill someone."

She continued to pace, visibly struggling with keeping it together.

"Jolie." Simon pushed himself to his feet and stepped into her path, bringing her up short and forcing her to look directly at him. "I don't know why you've been suffering from the blackouts, but I can promise you that we'll find out." When she would have turned away he took her by the arms and held her still. "I won't let anything else happen to you. You have my word on that. But I need you to trust me."

The fear in her eyes almost undid him completely. "Why would you do that?"

"Just trust me," he urged, not certain how much longer he could remain victorious over the war with his need to kiss her. To hold her.

She opened her mouth to argue, but apparently

thought better of it. "What happens now?" He heard the defeat in her tone.

"Now we act as if nothing has happened. And we pray Raymond Brasco, Sr., doesn't connect the murder of his only son to you."

She felt the fear claim her expression once more. "He'll kill me, won't he?"

Simon nodded. "He'll try."

She tossed her head, sending those silky blond tresses over her shoulder, and laughed, a sound filled with desperation and defeat. "None of this makes sense. It's crazy. Why would you risk your life for me?"

He stared at her lips as she spoke, fighting the urge to press his own there, to comfort her and make her forget. Or maybe to make him forget. "It doesn't matter why." He dragged his gaze upward to look directly into those jade pools of pure fear. "All you need to know is that I will."

Chapter Nine

Simon watched Jolie settle into her routine at the office on Monday morning. He wasn't thrilled at the idea of permitting her to come to work, but there was no way around it. She needed to work to get her mind off the events of the past week, and he needed her there to bait Boyer.

Simon hadn't allowed her out of his sight in the past twenty-four hours, insisting that she'd be safer at his place. His only concession to her wishes had been in accompanying her to her apartment to pick up clothes for the upcoming work week.

The message indicator light on her answering machine had flashed as they'd entered her silent apartment early Sunday afternoon. When Jolie pressed the button, the voice belonging to the dead guy she'd awakened next to had echoed in the thundering silence, sending sheer terror through her all over again. *Jolie...I'm waiting for you.*

Simon wadded the report in his hands. Fury charged through him. Someone was playing a game with her. A scenario had started to form late last night as he'd watched her sleep. He'd had to conquer the desire to lie next to her and hold her close, instead forcing his mind to focus on putting the pieces of this puzzle together.

Johnson had called demanding to know more, but Simon had no answers for him, only questions. Just as Simon had surmised, the restaurant Jolie frequented whenever she had the urge to go out to dinner, Carlisle's, was connected to Brasco and his empire. The owner, according to Johnson, was a distant cousin. Though Jolie had insisted that she hadn't accepted a drink from the man who joined her, she had consumed one glass of wine before his arrival. Had even recalled feeling dizzy and nauseated shortly afterward. Simon was certain she'd been drugged.

So certain, in fact, that he'd taken her by the home of a physician in the area he knew personally. Dr. Stewart had gladly accompanied them to his clinic and drawn a blood sample. He'd promised the results today.

Ray Brasco, Jr., had been watching Jolie. He'd known when she left for the restaurant. Had likely been parked near her apartment. The message left on her answering machine had come from a cellular telephone. Johnson had confirmed her number as showing up on the call log of the cell phone they'd found at the scene of the crime. Johnson had also confirmed Simon's belief that, if Jolie had been drugged, she could be innocent of the murder. The preliminary autopsy report, which had been expedited due to the victim's connection to the Bureau's ongoing case, had indicated that massive force was used in the stabbing, burying the knife blade to the hilt, even chipping a rib in the process. An angry woman, even one as slender and seemingly fragile as Jolie, would possess the necessary strength, but if she were under the influence of debilitating drugs, it was an unlikely scenario.

Simon remembered well how weak and vulnerable she'd been when he'd followed her from the restaurant the first time. He'd been convinced then that she had been drugged. He felt sure a blood test would have confirmed his conclusion had she not slipped away from him the next morning. At the time Simon hadn't considered the relevance of the restaurant, but now he knew differently. He didn't believe in coincidences. Jolie had been at Carlisle's that night, as well. Johnson was working on that angle. Since the restaurant was the last place the murder victim had been seen alive, the staff had been questioned. Only one staff member was unaccounted for—the waiter who'd served Jolie and Ray. Simon had a feeling that if they checked the waiter's schedule, they'd find he'd probably been on duty the last time Jolie patronized the establishment.

Simon's gaze followed her movements as she went about her day of overseeing international investments for the bank. Her position was perfect for laundering money. According to the bank president, both Jolie and Boyer had been up for the promotion, but Jolie had been the more qualified. Boyer hadn't shown any bitterness regarding the decision, at least none his boss noted.

Simon turned the possibilities over in his mind until he arrived at the most feasible scenario. Boyer was connected to Brasco; Simon had loosely established that much. However, he had also determined from the beginning that Boyer, in his capacity at the bank, could not have been laundering funds without Jolie's knowledge. That no longer felt right to Simon. He refused to acknowledge that his conclusion could have an emotional base. Instead, he enumerated the facts. Jolie held the necessary position, and somehow Boyer had used her to do what needed to be done. He'd fooled her or outright gone behind her back and simply hadn't gotten caught. But now things were different. She had either noticed the anomalies or suspected him, and he'd taken steps to set her up.

But that didn't explain the trip to the Cayman Islands. Or her total loss of memory regarding any suspicions, had there been any to begin with. Simon had another of the Colby Agency's investigators checking out that scenario right now. Pierce Maxwell—Max— had flown out yesterday to interview the staff at the bank where Jolie had supposedly set up the account. Simon would soon have some feedback on that score, as well.

Simon's cellular phone vibrated insistently. Anticipating the call, he flipped it open. "Ruhl."

"You hit the nail on the head." It was Dr. Stewart, the physician who'd agreed to obtain the lab work on Jolie's blood sample.

"What'd you find?" Simon needed specifics.

"Rohyphol—the date rape drug," Stewart reported, confirming Simon's suspicions. "I don't know how much you know about the drug, but it's about ten times as potent as Valium and has no taste or odor."

Simon absorbed the information, then asked, "Tell me about the side effects." He was aware of the most common—loss of inhibitions and the ability to reason.

"There's plenty," Stewart said grimly. "Impaired judgment as well as impaired motor skills. Renders a victim pretty much incapable of fighting off a physical attack. Blackouts lasting from eight to twenty-four hours. Lapses in memory, confusion. And even death if the dose is too high.''

Every symptom Jolie had suffered. Simon suddenly wondered if she'd somehow received smaller doses between the two main episodes. ''How long could the side effects last?''

The doctor made a noncommittal sound. ''Depending on the dosage the victim received, the mental confusion and a slight disorientation could last for days.''

Bingo.

''Thanks, Dr. Stewart. You've been a great help.''

Though Simon couldn't swear in a court of law that Jolie was entirely innocent, he did know that she had not been in complete possession of her mental faculties this past week. Considering the physical impairment the drug caused, he was now one hundred percent certain she couldn't have plunged that knife into Ray Brasco.

Anxious to pass along the information, Simon quickly punched in Johnson's number.

After listening to all that Simon had to say, Johnson related some news of his own. ''One of the neighbors that we couldn't catch up with yesterday finally got back into town today.''

Simon recalled that the older gentleman, Brasco's closest neighbor, had not been home yesterday when the local boys in blue had canvassed the apartment building.

''Had a family emergency and had to go out of town,'' Johnson explained. ''Anyway, as soon as he got back he called in. He claims that about two o'clock in the morning on Sunday he heard a hell of a ruckus coming from Brasco's place. Apparently, our vic and some female were arguing heatedly.''

A knot tied in Simon's gut. ''Anything else?''

''Nah. The old man shrugged it off and went to bed. Said that Brasco frequently got rowdy with his female visitors.''

That last part provided some sense of relief, but not much.

''Oh yeah,'' Johnson added. ''The forensics guys found a hair in the vic's right hand. Black in color, probably female.''

Johnson knew that Jolie was blond. Simon sensed that there was more. He could feel the tension vibrating over the phone line. He waited, his patience growing thinner by the second.

''There was pubic hair, too. Black also. Definitely female and Caucasian. Our vic apparently had himself a roll in the hay before buying the farm.''

Another emotion surged in Simon's chest. ''Miss Randolph is relatively certain she did not participate in any sexual activity with the victim.''

''But she isn't sure,'' Johnson prodded.

Simon clenched his jaw, sending a muscle there jerking rhythmically. Of course she couldn't be certain. Though if Brasco had raped her, he'd used a condom—that much she was certain of. She'd noticed no physical indications of sexual activity, but she'd refused to go through an examination when Dr. Stewart offered. She hadn't wanted to talk about any of it. Had flat out refused to discuss it further whenever Simon brought it up again.

''No,'' Simon admitted simply.

''All right. I'll give you more when I have it. But I warn you,'' Johnson added, ''I'm not going to be able to keep this under wraps long. She'll have to give a statement sooner or later.''

''You'll get your statement,'' Simon snapped. ''Is that all?''

The hesitation was answer enough. ''You're making a mistake, Simon,'' his old friend warned.

''Yeah, well, tell me something I don't know.'' He folded the cell phone, ending the discussion. He stared at the shiny mahogany surface of his desk and cursed himself yet again. Johnson was right. He was a fool. Simon resisted the urge to look up and see that Jolie was safe and sound in her office. He knew she was there—he could feel her presence even through the glass. He'd never felt this kind of need to be with someone.

The cell phone vibrated in his palm and he barely suppressed the urge to throw it across the room. Instead, he flipped down the mouthpiece and barked his usual greeting.

''It's Max. I've got an ID on the photograph you faxed me.''

Simon's instincts moved to a higher state of alert. ''A positive ID?'' That was the last thing he wanted to hear. Disappointment tugged at him.

''Not positive, but close. The president of the bank as well as one of the tellers remembers Miss Randolph. Neither of them would swear that the woman who set up the account was the woman in the photograph, but they were pretty sure. The hair's right, and the eyes. The height and weight match. But neither of them is absolutely certain.''

Simon rubbed a hand over his jaw. ''All right, Max. Thanks. Let me know if you learn anything new.''

"Will do."

Max had suggested that he do a little extra research in case Big Ray Brasco had any connections on Grand Cayman. Simon's gaze drifted to the woman across the hall. Could she have made the trip to the island and set up the account and have no recall whatsoever of doing it? And what about the transfers over the past three months? Could Boyer have somehow done those? Just when Simon was certain she was innocent, something else crawled out of the woodwork to bite him in the ass.

Maybe he was an even bigger fool than he knew.

JOLIE STUDIED the documents before her once more. She couldn't concentrate. She had to reread everything three times in order for the information to sink in.

It was no use. She closed her eyes and braced her head in her hands.

No matter how hard she tried she kept seeing that gruesome scene over and over in her head. The blood. The man's unseeing eyes wide open. The look of surprise permanently etched on his face. Jolie shuddered and her empty stomach threatened to revolt against her all over again.

She couldn't eat, she couldn't sleep. Every waking moment was consumed with fear and confusion. *Please, God,* she prayed for the thousandth time, *don't let me have had anything to do with that man's murder.*

She'd called her father last night, and the sound of his voice had been comforting to some degree. She'd wanted to tell him everything, to cry on his strong shoulder, but Simon had insisted that drawing him into this would only endanger his life. Jolie would die before she would do that. She'd lied and assured her father that everything was fine. Not one thing was the matter. She doubted he'd believed her, but he hadn't pressed the issue.

All she wanted was for things to go back to the way they were before.

The dark, alluring image of Simon Ruhl abruptly invaded her thoughts. If things went back to the way they were before, then Simon would be gone.

Drawing in a deep breath, she straightened in her chair and looked beyond the wall of glass to the man who had rescued her, at least temporarily. He appeared to be deep in conversation with someone on his cellular phone. She took the moment to study him more closely. It wasn't often that she could get a glimpse of the enigmatic man without his knowledge. The strength and power he emanated made her feel safe and protected. That he was handsome in a sinfully dark way made her feel restless for the first time in a very long time. She couldn't even remember the last time she'd been so attracted to anyone.

She wanted desperately to believe that his intentions were noble, that he wanted first and foremost to help her. He'd told her that the board of directors suspected Mark Boyer of criminal activities and that perhaps he was somehow using Jolie to accomplish that end. But she couldn't help worrying that Simon wasn't telling her everything.

Drugs had never been her thing, not even as a teenager. She'd been a Goody two-shoes her whole life. But for the first time ever she prayed that drugs were the cause of her confusion and lapses in memory. If the blood test came back positive for drugs, then maybe she could breathe easier about her mental well-being. Simon had told her if she had been drugged with the substance he suspected, the lingering side effects would only be temporary. Once the drug was completely out of her system she should be her old self again.

She allowed that tiny seed of hope to sprout and bloom inside her. It was something to hold on to. Just like Simon. He looked up then, his gaze locking instantly with hers, sending butterflies into flight in her tummy. The sensation was definitely much more pleasant than the one she'd been experiencing all morning. She told herself not to get overly infatuated with the man. He was here to do a job, and he would be leaving. And she might very well be spending the rest of her life in prison.

She looked away first, unable to hold that intense eye contact. Instinct told her that he felt something for her, that he wanted to protect her, but reason scolded her and warned her that he was only doing his job.

Too weary to consider the confusing aspects of her life any further, she forced her mind to refocus on the accounts spread across her desk. She had a job to do, as well.

"Knock, knock, busy lady."

Startled, Jolie looked up at the sound of Erica's voice. The familiar face of her friend brought a smile to Jolie's lips. "Erica! What're you doing here?"

Erica met her halfway around her desk and gave her a hug. "Well, Renae told me you'd be too busy to go out for lunch today, so I brought lunch to you."

Jolie frowned, then grinned when her friend pointed to the waiter pushing a serving cart up the corridor in the direction of Jolie's office. "You didn't," she countered, not quite believing her eyes.

Erica winked. "I did."

The waiter stationed the cart in the middle of Jolie's office, bowed gracefully and exited without a word.

Lifting the lid from one of the covered dishes, Erica announced, "Your favorite, Florentine rice and chicken, steamed vegetables, and…" she waved toward the accompanying carafe "…unsweetened tea."

"Thanks." Jolie gave her another hug. "You don't know how much I needed a distraction today." She refused to look in Simon's direction again. She needed this moment of escape from it all.

Once they'd poured the tea and filled their plates, Erica demanded, "All right, what's going on? You leave me a message to meet you at Carlisle's on Saturday night. When I got home on Sunday afternoon—" she waggled her brows suggestively "—don't ask where I spent the night, you're nowhere to be found. I must have called your house a dozen times last night."

Jolie played with her food, picking at it instead of eating it despite the incredibly delicious aroma. How could she have an appetite after all that had happened? "I spent the night at my father's," she said, lying for the second time in the past twenty-four hours. "I didn't feel like being alone." That part, at least, was the truth. Her whole life was falling apart. She blinked back the tears that blurred her vision. She would not cry.

Erica set her fork aside and took Jolie's hand. "Honey, you've got to let me help. I don't know what's going on, but after what you told me the other day I believe you should get professional help.''

Jolie peered helplessly at her friend. Even Erica believed she was losing it. ''I don't know what to do.'' She wanted so much to tell her it had happened again, and about the man—the murdered man. But Simon had ordered her not to say a word to anyone. She definitely didn't want to endanger Erica's life, but she so needed her friend right now.

Erica took a resolute breath and nodded. ''All right. It's bigger than the two of us. Whatever happened to you, we need someone to get to the bottom of it. I think you should see a shrink and have hypnosis.''

The suggestion startled Jolie, but it gave her pause, as well. ''Do you think that would work?''

Erica shrugged. ''I don't know why not. If the shrink can take you back in time and walk you through that night, then you'll know what happened and who you were with.''

Too late, Jolie mused. She already knew where she'd spent the night, but she couldn't tell her friend that, either.

''I guess it'd be worth a try,'' Jolie hedged, not sure how Simon would feel about the suggestion.

''Darn right it would,'' Erica reiterated. ''I want my friend back.'' She squeezed Jolie's hand. ''The one who smiled and told me all her secrets.''

Jolie laughed nervously. Was she that easy to read? ''You know I've never had any secrets from you.''

Erica patted her hand and sighed. ''I know. Because we're friends. I don't want to see you like this, Jolie.''

By mutual unspoken consent they turned their attention back to the lovely ''to go'' lunch nearby Lebron's restaurant had prepared. Jolie so appreciated the gesture. But she couldn't tell Erica any more than she had. Thankfully, her friend seemed to sense and understand that boundary.

A few minutes later Erica made a sound of satisfaction and insisted she was stuffed. "I should go." She set her plate and glass on the cart. "The waiter will come back in an hour or so and take this away." She winked. "He's kind of cute, don't you think?"

Truthfully, Jolie hadn't even noticed, but she smiled and nodded. She put her plate and glass on the cart, as well. "Thank you again for making my day," she said in all sincerity. "I feel tons better now."

Erica reached for her hand and gave it another squeeze. "Call me tonight, okay?"

Jolie nodded.

When she would have released her, Erica stared at Jolie's hand, a frown marring her expression. "Where's your watch?"

Jolie looked down at her left wrist. The gold watch her father had given her was missing. She'd worn it to work on Friday; she remembered that clearly. Saturday and Sunday were a bit of a blur. Maybe she'd left it at home on her bedside table Saturday morning.

The memory of checking it at the restaurant as she waited zoomed to the forefront of her thoughts. She'd had it on at the restaurant Saturday night. She'd been without it at Simon's apartment. That could mean only one thing....

She'd lost it at the dead man's apartment.

Chapter Ten

"I searched the apartment thoroughly," Simon told her once more. "The watch was not there."

Jolie shook her head adamantly. "It has to be. I had it on that night."

He understood what she was going through, but she had to trust him. If the watch had been found, Johnson would have told him. The forensic techs had swept the apartment twice already. "You must have lost it somewhere before you reached Brasco's apartment. The watch definitely wasn't there."

Jolie rubbed her left wrist, as if touching the spot the watch had last been would somehow give her insight as to where it was now. "Well...I guess it'll turn up."

She looked so confused. Again his protective instincts surged, willing him to take her into his arms and hold her until her fears subsided. But he couldn't do that. He was way over the line already.

"Just stay calm," he suggested. "Boyer's bound to make a move sooner or later."

Jolie shook her head and waved her hands in resignation. "I just can't see it." She started to pace, her usual response to a stressful situation. "You keep telling me that Mark is somehow setting me up, and I simply can't believe it. We worked side by side for years. I know him." She paused and looked straight at Simon. "He's not that kind of guy. He's…" She shrugged. "I don't know, he's sort of a wimp. I can't see him with mobsters. He's no tough guy and certainly no mastermind behind some plot to launder money for the mob."

She could be right in some respects. The man she thought she knew might not be capable of those things, but that didn't mean he allowed her to see who he really was.

"Jolie." She shivered visibly. From all the stress, Simon presumed. A part of him wanted to believe that it was because she felt the same attraction to him that he felt for her. Who the hell was he kidding? He knew she was attracted to him, but he also knew that it could be a part of her vulnerability rather than true chemistry. "You know what Boyer has allowed you to know. You can't be certain what he's capable of."

She shook her head in denial. "I just don't see how he could pull it all off. Surely I wouldn't be that blind."

Simon couldn't say what she wanted to hear. She was searching for some sense in all this and there simply was none. "Let's take this apart one piece at a time." He sat down on the edge of the conference table and gestured for her to take a seat. Reluctantly she obliged. "You have the overriding access to all accounts for the bank's foreign investors, right?"

"Yes. *Me*, not Mark," she emphasized.

"If Boyer were to somehow gain access to your password, he could literally do anything you could, right?"

Jolie stiffened a bit. "Well, yes, but—"

"But nothing. That's the case and you know it. Whether with your permission or without it, if he has gained access to your password, he can transfer the funds of your accounts anywhere he chooses, leaving you to believe that you'd done it and forgotten about it."

A troubling frown marred her brow as she considered Simon's theory. Though it was far from fully fleshed out, it was more than plausible. "I don't understand what that would accomplish."

Simon exhaled a heavy breath. "That's the missing piece of the puzzle. We don't know the motivation. If he has been laundering money, which he can already do from his current position to a large extent, then there's no reason for this sudden sloppiness."

"You mean the foreign account in my name and the obviously embezzled funds," she supplied.

He nodded. "That was a blatant attempt to throw suspicion of wrongdoing on you. The question is why." Simon considered the theories he'd toyed with. "It would get you out of the way and him a promotion, but why bother if he's been taking care of business all along? There are only two logical possibilities that I can come up with."

Jolie sat on the edge of her seat, waiting for his next words. Those green eyes were wide with hope, and her lush lips parted slightly in anticipation. His body hardened with need and he had to look away.

"One," he stated before he lost focus entirely, "Brasco has gotten wind of the investigation and Boyer wants to throw the feds off his scent. If he needs this bank, then he may be hoping a huge embezzlement scandal involving you would shift the scrutiny.''

Jolie chewed her lower lip while she mulled over that possibility. ''What's the second theory?''

Simon held her gaze again as he said what he considered to be the most likely scenario. ''I think this is personal. Boyer wants you out of the picture and he intends to do it any way he can. Maybe losing the promotion made him look bad to Brasco. Bottom line, I think he wants you out and he's setting you up to take a big fall.''

Her breath caught. ''You…think he put that man up to call me and pretend he knew me, then he killed him.'' Her hand went to her mouth, horror and disbelief written all over her face.

''Maybe. Since you discovered the embezzled funds and made the changes before anyone noticed, maybe he sought another route to get rid of you. If he could make Brasco think that you'd killed his son, he wouldn't have to worry about getting you out of the way, Brasco would take care of it for him. He must have somehow tricked Ray, Jr., into going along with him.''

Having recovered from the momentary shock, Jolie pushed herself to her feet, shaking her head in adamant denial once more. ''You don't know Mark like I do. That's impossible! He wouldn't hurt a fly, much less kill a human being.'' She folded her arms over her chest in punctuation of her words. ''No, it's just not possible. I know him. He couldn't do it.''

''For your sake, I hope you're wrong.'' Simon locked his gaze with hers. ''Because if it's not him, then it would have to be *you*. My friend in the Bureau is keeping your name out of this murder investigation for the time being, but he won't be able to do it for long. If Brasco thinks you're the one who killed his son, he'll want revenge."

Simon saw another shiver run through her, this one motivated by fear. "You told me I couldn't have done it, considering the drug that had been used to sedate me. Won't that make a difference?"

Simon pressed her with his gaze once more, hoping to relay the lethal certainty of his words. "Raymond Brasco won't be interested in excuses or even in listening to reason. He won't care what the circumstances were. If you were with his son when he was murdered, then you're guilty in his book."

Jolie looked away. She didn't want to hear the truth. But Simon had to make her understand. "Listen to me, Jolie, you have to watch your step from this moment forward. I'll protect you, you have my word on that, but I don't think you fully comprehend what kind of threat Brasco represents."

She held up her hands. "I get the picture. And I have work to do."

She walked out of the conference room without looking back. Simon watched her until she was safely settled behind her desk in her own office. He wished he could save her from what was to come, but even he couldn't perform miracles. And it would take a miracle—the resurrection of his son, to be precise—to stave off Brasco's vengeance.

Now seemed like the right time to lean a little heavier on Boyer, Simon decided.

As he passed Jolie's office he stopped in and warned her not to go anywhere without him. She rolled her eyes and turned back to her work. He reasoned that denial was her only protection from the harsh reality of what was happening around her, but denial could get her into serious trouble.

"Yes, sir, I'm happy to assist you." Boyer looked up from his telephone conversation and motioned for Simon to come into his office.

Rather than take the seat Boyer offered with a wave of his hand, Simon moved around the small office, looking at the plaques proclaiming Boyer's excellence in the business of investments and financial advising. Simon wondered if he'd intended to keep for himself the money he'd embezzled in Jolie's name. Though he had no concrete proof of his theory, Simon's instincts told him he was right. Still, he would need hard evidence to back it up. To get that evidence he needed to rattle Boyer's cage. Send him running to Brasco for help. Because Simon's agenda was still the same: getting the goods on Raymond Brasco, Sr.

"Please, Mr. Ruhl, have a seat," Boyer offered the moment he'd finished his call.

Simon turned to him and smiled. "Actually, I have a couple of questions for you."

"Shoot," Boyer said, still smiling like a used car salesman hoping to make his quota for the week.

Simon dropped into one of the upholstered chairs flanking his desk. "Were you here at the bank this weekend?"

The question took Boyer by surprise. "Working, you mean?" he inquired, as if he wasn't sure what Simon meant by the question.

"Yes." He nodded. "Working. There were a number of transactions that struck me as odd. Two involved the First Royal Cayman Bank."

Boyer recovered quickly, but Simon didn't miss the flare of surprise that registered briefly in his eyes. The banker pursed his lips and pretended to give it some thought. "No," he finally said, shaking his head. "I don't handle any accounts with that bank. You should talk to Jolie—she may have one or two." He tapped his chin. "In fact, I think I recall her taking a trip to the islands a couple of months back. Business, I believe." He nodded thoughtfully. "Yes, definitely, you should speak with her about that bank."

Boyer was a good liar, but not good enough. The feds had already traced a numbered account at a Swiss bank to him. No way would his salary allow for that kind of cumulative savings. He was definitely doing something illegal. All that remained was tying him to Brasco.

"You didn't answer my question," Simon accused.

"I beg your pardon." He looked visibly shaken this time. Maybe Jolie was right. Perhaps Boyer didn't possess the nerves of steel required to choreograph this kind of setup. He certainly didn't appear the type to handle major business deals with a man like Raymond Brasco.

"Did you work this weekend? I'm sure the security logs will verify if you came into the bank."

"Yes. Of course," he rushed to clarify. "I work Saturdays quite often."

"That's all I needed to know." Simon stood and produced a smile for the nervous man. "Thanks for your cooperation."

He walked out, knowing he'd accomplished his mission. Boyer was definitely rattled.

"MISS RANDOLPH."

Jolie looked up from her work as Renae rushed into

her office, arms loaded with files. "Yes, Renae, what can I do for you?"

"Mr. Knox called from EastTrust and needs you to join him in a meeting there right away." She balanced the folders in one arm and handed Jolie the one on top with her free hand. "He'd like you to bring over this file."

Jolie skirted her desk and took the folder, automatically reading the name on the file. "Sure. I'll go right over."

"He's waiting," Renae added for good measure, before she scurried away.

Jolie wondered why Mr. Knox would go to a meeting at another bank to discuss the Fairfax account without consulting with her first. It was, after all, her account. To her knowledge the Fairfax Group did no business with EastTrust. Maybe that was about to change. The possibility that she might be about to lose the account niggled at the edge of her thoughts, but she pushed it away. She'd had that account for five years. If there was a problem the client would have let her know.

Smoothing a hand over her navy skirt, Jolie reached for her jacket and slipped into it. She reclaimed the file and snagged her purse. Mr. Knox did not like to be kept waiting. As she zoomed out of her office she remembered Simon's warning for her not to go anywhere without him.

For about three seconds she deliberated on the point, then she stuck her head into the conference room. He was in the middle of what sounded like a heated debate.

"No, that's not what I said," he argued into his cell phone.

She waved to get his attention.

He looked up, held up his hand for her to give him a minute, and then was quickly dragged back into the conversation. "No." He shook his head, his jaw clenched so tightly a muscle jumped there, almost distracting Jolie from her mission. His chiseled good looks were enough to throw any woman off balance.

When he didn't look up again, she turned and left. Mr. Knox was waiting. EastTrust was only three blocks up the street. She'd be fine. She wasn't really worried about Brasco at this point. Her name had been kept out of the investigation. And if Mark was the evil link, as Simon had suggested, she didn't have to worry about him, either, because he was in conference with a client in his office. She shivered when she recalled Simon's pointed statement in response to her insistence that it couldn't possibly be Mark. *Then it would have to be you.* It wasn't her. And it wasn't Mark. She shook off the lingering doubts. She had a meeting to get to.

She would be fine.

Ten minutes later Jolie stood before the desk of the secretary to the president of EastTrust Bank and felt her confusion mounting.

"You're certain Mr. Knox isn't here," she repeated, knowing how foolish she sounded. She'd already asked twice, and the secretary was clearly losing her patience.

"Yes, Miss Randolph. I'm quite certain." To the lady's credit she kept her smile in place and her tone accommodating.

Jolie shook her head, utterly baffled. This was ridiculous. Renae never made mistakes like this. "I guess there was a miscommunication."

"Would you like to call your assistant?" the secretary offered.

"Yes, please."

The secretary pointed to a telephone on a nearby side table. "Just dial nine to get out."

Jolie punched in the number of the bank and waited to be transferred to Mr. Knox's office. She decided to go straight to the source. When his secretary answered, she asked, "Charlotte, the meeting Mr. Knox asked me to join—which bank was it?"

"Miss Randolph, I'm afraid you've caught me at a disadvantage. What meeting are you talking about and what time was it scheduled for?"

Jolie looked at the file again, suddenly not trusting her eyes or her ears. "The Fairfax meeting he's in right now. Renae said—"

"Mr. Knox isn't in a meeting," she interrupted, her tone reflecting her own confusion. Everyone got nervous when a scheduling glitch reared its ugly head. "He had to be worked in at his dentist's office. A crown popped off at breakfast this morning. He's only supposed to be gone for about forty-five minutes. Do you need to see him when he returns?"

A tendril of fear curled in Jolie's middle. "What time is the Fairfax meeting scheduled for?"

Jolie heard the clicking of keys as Charlotte checked the electronic calendar. "There is no Fairfax meeting. Is there another subject it might be listed as, maybe?"

"Never mind. Thank you." Jolie hung up the phone, her mind whirling with questions. Why would Renae give her the wrong information? Was she working for Mark? Were they in this together?

"Did you find out where you're supposed to be?" the secretary asked, jolting Jolie back to the present.

She managed a smile. "Yes. Thank you."

Struggling with the urge to run, Jolie walked out of the bank. She had to stay calm. They were both against her—Mark and Renae. The concept kept playing over and over in her head: *Simon was right.* This wasn't about her mother or her illness. This was about greed and betrayal.

Her fury as well as her paranoia complete now, Jolie marched up the sidewalk toward Atlanta's First International Bank. When she got back to her office she was simply going to confront Mark and Renae. She would have the truth now. Today! She wasn't going to live in fear a moment longer. She didn't need the shrink Erica had suggested, nor was she suffering from stress overload as her father feared. She was being used. She'd blindly trusted those around her and look where it had gotten her.

When Jolie would have turned the corner to the bank, she caught a glimpse of movement coming from the rear entrance on the opposite side of the street. Renae was hurrying down the walk on that side of the street, so intent on her destination that she didn't bother looking up. Fury enveloped Jolie all over again. Was she going to meet Mark in some out of the way place to discuss how they'd fooled Jolie yet again? How they'd made her think she was losing her mind one more time?

Giving Renae a generous head start, Jolie stealthily followed. She stayed close to the buildings, allowing the late-lunch crowd to shield her from sight in the event that Renae might look behind her. Jolie's anticipation as well as her anger built steadily with every step she took. All she could think about was how much she'd trusted these people. They were supposed to be her friends.

Four minutes later Renae entered Lebron's. Jolie gave her time to be escorted from the waiting area and then she entered as well.

"A table for one?" the hostess asked, smiling brightly, immediately recognizing Jolie as a regular lunch patron.

"No." Jolie didn't spare her more than a fleeting glance. "I'm looking for someone. I'll only be here a moment."

She moved through the restaurant, using plants and people, whatever was handy, for camouflage as necessary. Finally she saw Renae at a table. Her back was to Jolie, so she wouldn't see her watching. Jolie's heart thudded, making her chest ache with each breath she dragged in. If only the waiter would move, Jolie would be able to see who sat at the table with her assistant. God, if it was Mark, would she be able to walk away without confronting them right here, right now?

The waiter stepped away, and Jolie's gaze riveted to the second person at the table.

The heavy-set, older woman laughed at something Renae said, and Jolie instantly recognized her as Renae's mother.

She closed her eyes and exhaled a mountain of tension. Before she could be seen and humiliated further, she turned and left the restaurant.

However Renae had gotten the misinformation about Mr. Knox, it was unintentional. Jolie railed silently at herself as she slowly walked back toward the bank. How ridiculous that she would have suspected

Renae! This whole thing was making her paranoid. And it was all Simon's fault. She'd told him that Mark couldn't be behind all this, and he wouldn't believe her. He'd pushed the issue until she was seeing bad guys at every turn.

It was ridiculous.

Renae was no more guilty of betrayal than Jolie was of murder. She shuddered at the thought. How could any of this be real? She was just an ordinary person. She had no connections to crime or anyone involved in crime. She'd never had so much as a parking ticket in her entire life. This wasn't supposed to happen to someone who played by the rules.

Jolie shivered with the reality of what she was facing. Who could she trust? Simon? Mr. Knox? Renae…maybe? She couldn't be sure of anything. She hugged her arms around herself, suddenly cold despite the warm temperature. The lunch crowd had pretty much dispersed, heading back to their offices. She felt acutely, inexplicably alone walking down that final stretch of sidewalk before she reached the rear entrance of the bank. Atlanta was a thriving, perpetually growing metropolis. She wasn't supposed to feel alone here…but she did.

The unmistakable roar of an engine abruptly blasted the quiet. Jolie looked up just in time to see a black sedan barreling directly at her.

She froze.

For a full second she was certain it must be a mistake or a dream. Two wheels left the street and bounced onto the sidewalk, the car headed straight at her.

She had to run.

But her legs were like leaden clubs sinking into the mire the sidewalk beneath her had instantly become.

She couldn't move.

The luxury emblem on the vehicle's front grill held her in a kind of trance.

She was going to die.

Strong arms suddenly encircled her and whisked her off her feet.

The next thing she knew she was on the ground.

Simon Ruhl hovered over her, demanding to know if she was all right. Worry twisted the features of his handsome face.

She tried to answer, but she couldn't speak.

And then the world, including Simon, went away.

Chapter Eleven

"I've never fainted in my life."

Jolie sat on the edge of Simon's sofa, her skirt and blouse wrinkled and soiled where she'd lain on the ground in that alley. Her shredded panty hose had been pitched aside, along with her high heel shoes and her jacket. Both knees were scraped, but lucky for her, that was the extent of her injuries. Simon struggled to keep his emotions in check. She'd been through enough; he didn't want to upset her more. But she'd almost gotten herself killed by not following his instructions. For that he wanted to shake her—but resisted, just barely. Besides, he was as much to blame as she was.

"Let me get something for those scrapes," he said with more calm than he had a right to possess at the moment. If he'd listened when she'd tried to get his attention, this wouldn't have happened. But he'd been too caught up in a battle with Johnson, who'd wanted to bring her in today. Simon had once allowed the black-and-white of the system's bureaucracy to dictate his every move. A frown wrinkled his brow. Funny thing was, he didn't remember exactly when that had changed. Recently, he decided, his gaze settling on Jolie. Very recently.

Finally Johnson had conceded and given him just forty-eight hours to bring her in. Simon bit back an oath. Somehow he had to have a break in the case before then.

"I don't understand what happened," she continued, as if he hadn't said a word. "That driver…" She shook her head. "He must have been drunk or…or something."

When she lapsed into silence, Simon went in search of the needed supplies to treat her abrasions. She was kidding herself. Though he dreaded her reaction, he'd have to tear down that defensive mechanism and make her see the truth. That car careening onto the sidewalk was no accident.

Quickly locating the first aid kit he always packed for assignments, he moved back to the living room and knelt down before her. She didn't move or speak as he opened the kit and removed the items he needed. Foolishly, he wished he could simply let her believe what she would. She was already so vulnerable. But that would be too dangerous for her. She wasn't a child. She could handle the truth. He just didn't want to be the one who shattered that final cocooning layer of innocence she'd managed to hang on to all these years.

He cursed himself now for harboring a single doubt about her innocence in all this. Despite the evidence that she couldn't have killed Ray, Jr., and her continued denial that Mark Boyer was involved in wrongdoing—all of which pointed to her complete obliviousness to any sort of illegal activities at the bank—he'd still chosen to follow her after she'd left

EastTrust. The moment he'd realized she wasn't in her office he'd gone in search of her. Renae had told him she was to meet Mr. Knox at EastTrust. But when Simon had arrived at the location, she'd been on her way out. Rather than make his presence known, he'd followed her just to be certain.

Jolie winced at the sting of the antiseptic, jerking Simon from his self-deprecating thoughts. "Sorry," he muttered. Damn it, how had he let his emotions get control of this case? He hadn't been thinking straight for days now. If he hadn't been so determined to prove he was wrong about her, he wouldn't have had any doubts. His gut had told him all along that she was innocent. Too bad his heart and his brain couldn't get together on the issue. He released a disgusted sigh as he finished up. He understood perfectly the problem, he just didn't want to admit it. He'd fallen for the woman, but a part of him rebelled at the idea of confessing to breaking his number one rule: never get involved with a client or a suspect.

He'd watched his peers at the Colby Agency fall in love one by one, and he'd sworn that would never happen to him—not on the job, anyway. He'd allowed emotions to rule him on one other occasion and had suffered the devastating effects. Yet here he was, doing exactly the same thing.

"That should do it." He packed away the supplies and pushed to his feet. "I'll get you something to drink and then we can talk about what happened."

"Simon."

"I'll be right back," he said, without sparing her a glance. He needed a minute to pull himself back together. A minute that included some distance between them.

Once in the privacy of his room he tossed the kit onto the dresser and then braced his hands there. He stared at his reflection. ''What the hell are you doing?'' he demanded of the man he scarcely recognized staring back at him.

It wasn't as if he hadn't taken an emotional tumble before. He had. He'd gotten over it without any bitterness or cynicism. He had his share of female companionship, as his schedule permitted. His life was far from lacking socially. The truth was he had an active sex life, a great job, good friends. What was the problem? He hadn't sworn off love or avoided it; he simply hadn't fallen for anyone else after that first time. He assumed he would one day when he crossed paths with the right woman. It just wasn't supposed to be like this. He'd allowed emotions to get in the way of work once before, and his partner had paid the price. It wasn't supposed to happen again. Simon was supposed to be smarter than that.

But then, this wasn't about falling in love, it was about being stupid. And he'd turned stupid way too fast on this one.

He had one shot at Big Ray Brasco and this was it. If he screwed it up he'd never forgive himself. During his last conversation with Johnson, the agent had related Brasco's reaction as he'd learned about the death of his son. The older man would be emotionally distraught now, increasing the likelihood of mistakes. Simon had to be prepared. It was hard to garner any sympathy for the man even now. According to Johnson, the son had been every bit as evil as his father. But no one deserved to be murdered, Simon admitted. Not even the scum of the earth. Still, the situation did present the advantage of catching

Brasco in a vulnerable position. Now was not the time to go soft or to lose focus.

Simon's conscience screamed indignantly, reminding him that the woman in the other room was depending on him, as well. If he screwed up she would be caught in the middle. The question was, did he want Brasco badly enough to sacrifice her safety? To use her as bait? Brasco wouldn't be able to resist if he knew....

The hesitation Simon experienced before reaching the right decision made him sick to his stomach. He turned away from the mirror. The bile of self-disgust burned in his throat when he realized how badly the need for vengeance had skewed his judgment. For days now he'd struggled to find a balance between what he felt for Jolie and how badly he wanted to bring down Brasco. Simon was supposed to be one of the good guys. He'd sworn long ago that he didn't have a price, that nothing but truth and justice could buy his allegiance. But he'd been wrong. He did have a price. His price was getting even.

The worst part was he'd almost allowed Jolie to be the one to pay.

All because he wanted so desperately to crack this case that he'd doubted her when every instinct had warned him that she was innocent.

"Simon."

His head came up at the sound of her voice. Barefoot, her hair tousled, she stood in the doorway, looking uncertain and vulnerable. If she only knew.

"Yeah?" He straightened, pushing away the truth he refused to accept. He was one of the good guys. He wouldn't let the vengeance burning inside him take over. Being human was his one insurmountable weakness, but being a man of his word and a Colby agent was the reason he wouldn't fail to do the right thing. "You okay?"

She shrugged halfheartedly, then looked into his eyes. "Are you?"

JOLIE KNEW SOMETHING was very wrong. In the week she'd known Simon he had been strong, confident, driven even. But now he was quiet, withdrawn. For the first time since they'd met she was certain she'd seen fear in his eyes. When she'd awakened in his arms in that alley, he'd looked frantic, almost hysterical. It didn't make sense. He'd insisted on bringing her home—to his home—right away. She'd barely talked him out of a trip to the hospital. She was fine, just shaken. The idea that she'd fainted had given her a fright, but otherwise she was okay. Accidents happened. That she'd survived it with nothing but skinned knees was a good thing, to her way of thinking. It had scared the hell out of her. She'd fainted! But now, in retrospect, she was just so damned glad to be alive. The idea that she'd come close to dying arranged everything into clearer focus.

But Simon obviously had something else on his mind or simply didn't see it that way.

When a response wasn't forthcoming, she moved close to him and asked again, "Is everything okay?"

He looked away, another first. She'd always been the one to cave under the intensity of those dark eyes. For some reason the tables had turned.

"I made a mistake."

She flinched at his harsh tone, but the ache that underscored it drew her another step closer. "What kind of mistake?" She tried to keep her attention focused fully on the discussion, but when she was this close to him it was just too hard. Her gaze drifted down to his black shirt and the matching tie he'd pulled loose at some point during all the excitement. She suddenly wondered why he always wore black. Not that she minded; the look was definitely sexy on him. But she wanted to know more about him. To understand what made this enigmatic man tick.

No. What she really wanted was to forget. To forget that she'd almost been killed by some careless driver. To forget that she'd awakened in bed with a dead man just days ago. The foreign account, the unexplained transfer deposits—all of it was just too much. She needed to forget all that…to pretend it away for just a little while.

"I should get you that drink," he said, drawing her gaze back to his face, which had an even more devastating effect on her nervous system. It wasn't just the way he looked, it was the way he spoke, the way he moved. She wanted to know him….

Jolie couldn't say what possessed her at that moment, but she suddenly decided that the time to know him better—a lot better—was now. She'd been fighting the attraction to him for days. She didn't want to fight anymore. She didn't want to think about money laundering or death or careless drivers anymore. She wanted to forget everything but touching Simon. She reached for the tie and pulled it free of his shirt.

"I don't want a drink," she told him, feeling in control for the first time in days. "I want you." This new boldness gave her a sense of power she'd never before experienced. Desire surged through her, emboldening her all the more. She released a couple of shirt buttons, revealing a V of bronzed skin. Her breath caught as her fingertips grazed that smooth terrain. She remembered seeing him shirtless that one time, and how beautifully sculpted his torso had looked. She wanted to feel the ridges and planes, feel those strong arms around her, and that was just the beginning. Her heart bumped erratically against her sternum.

"Jolie." He pulled her hands away from the task of unbuttoning his shirt. "You're not thinking straight. This would be—"

"Right," she interrupted as she lifted her face to his, forcing him to look directly into her eyes. "Please, Simon, I don't want to think anymore. I just want to feel."

He wanted her to. She could see it in his eyes, in the way he looked at her mouth now. He wanted to kiss her. She wanted it more. Going up on tiptoe, she brushed her lips against his, feeling his breath catch, as her own did the same.

She felt his surrender, nothing more than a subtle shift in his posture, but a monumental step for a man who played by the rules. Releasing her wrists, those strong hands cupped her face, his thumbs stroking her cheeks as he drew out the moment. Finally his mouth claimed hers and all else ceased to matter. Firm and yet somehow soft, his lips moved over hers, touching, tasting and finally possessing completely. Her heart fluttered wildly in her breast as his hands moved downward to trace her body, to learn her as she so desperately yearned to know him…urging her toward the escape she sought.

Following his lead, she smoothed her palms down his chest, but it wasn't enough. She needed to touch his skin, flesh against flesh. She tugged at the buttons of his shirt, releasing some, sending others flying to the floor. And then she touched him. Her hands splayed over his warm muscled chest and want throbbed deep inside her. She couldn't remember the last time she'd been like this with a man. Touching Simon and feeling his hands on her as he eased her blouse off her shoulders overshadowed all other sexual moments she'd ever experienced. It was at once intense and tender. No other man had touched her this way.

Her bra disappeared and his mouth was suddenly on her breast. He suckled deeply, falling to his knees before her with a groan of need so savage that the very sound almost sent her over the edge. She clung to his broad shoulders, helpless to do anything but revel in the feel of his wicked tongue, his hot steamy mouth. He laved her breasts, each in turn, until she cried out with need. She wanted to tell him to hurry, but she couldn't find the words, she could only surrender to every touch of his lips and hands. The pleasure cascading through her was too much, the want too strong.

He stripped off her skirt, then slowly, so very slowly, dragged her panties down her thighs. She watched his expression, so intent on the task, as he revealed the part of her that ached for his touch…the only part of her that he had not touched. The panties dropped to her ankles as he kissed her intimately, starting a new kind of frenzy. She closed her eyes as the unexpected explosion started. Wave after wave of release quaked through her and still he didn't stop the sweet invasion. How could he do that with nothing more than his hands? His oh-so-talented mouth? Before she could catch her breath, he was easing her down onto the bed. Somehow he had undressed while she'd floated on that sensuous cloud of sensation. His bare skin felt hot and smooth against her. She wanted to touch him all over.

She twined her legs with his, urging him into the cradle of her thighs, needing to feel him inside her. But he hesitated, took his time kissing her as if they had forever. When he'd taken his fill of her mouth he moved back to her breasts. He tugged at one already tender nipple with his teeth, and she cried out his name. Desperate for more, she plunged her fingers into his thick hair and urged him on. He didn't disappoint her. His hot mouth moved over her skin, taking in a generous portion of her other waiting breast. He sucked hard. She screamed with the first contraction of her feminine muscles.

How could he draw her to a climax again so quickly? Before a reasonable explanation could fully form, he moved downward, rekindling the fire, which seared even deeper than before. Her whole body went rigid. She couldn't take anymore. She needed him to finish this.

"No more," she urged, tugging him upward. When his gaze locked with hers, she told him with her eyes what she couldn't form the words to say.

He obeyed, moving over her as fluidly as liquid heat, the fire in his eyes melting her heart, binding her to him with the first thrust of his lean hips. He filled her so completely she wanted to weep. His savage groan as his eyes closed in that same ecstasy sent sheer pleasure soaring through her. Then the plunge toward release began again. His movements frantic, his need perfectly matching her own, he drove them over the edge. They fell together with a simultaneous cry of fulfillment.

As the flood of sensation slowly receded, Jolie knew that she would never know a moment like this with anyone else. Because there was no one else on the planet like Simon Ruhl.

How would she ever let him go when this was over?

SIMON REMAINED STRANGELY quiet as he prepared an early dinner for the two of them. He'd insisted that she sit, relax and allow him to take care of everything. How could she relax? She wanted to scream in frustration. They'd just shared the single most sexually gratifying moment of her life, and he had nothing to say. But she sensed it was more than post-sex awkwardness.

Realization hit her with all the force of a physical blow. He regretted their lovemaking. He was an investigator and she was part of his case. He'd broken some stupid rule and now he was sorry about it.

"You're angry that this happened," she said, determined to have it out in the open.

His hands stilled in their work of arranging the makings of a salad, but he said nothing.

Jolie nodded, more an acknowledgment to herself than to him. She was right. At least he wasn't going to deny it. "That's great." She scooted off the stool and smoothed a nonexistent wrinkle from her slacks. The fabric chaffed the skin still tender from her up-close encounter with the ground, but she'd had to choose from the clothes she'd brought to Simon's to wear to work this week. She'd showered and changed, trashing the navy suit that had been one of her favorites, and applied more ointment to her scrapes. The bruises surfacing would take time to fade. But all in all, she felt extremely fortunate to be alive. However, that didn't lessen the hurt or the blow to her ego Simon's continued silence imparted. "I need to go home."

That remark brought his head up, that dark, penetrating gaze cutting right through her. "You know I can't let you out of my sight."

She resisted the urge to curl her fingers into fists. She'd had a bad day that appeared bent on only getting worse, and she needed some time alone. It wasn't a request, it was a demand. Though her heart wouldn't allow her to regret what they'd shared, another part of her deeply mourned his obvious regret. "I can stay with my father." She glanced around the room. What had she done with her purse? The living room, maybe. She could stop by her apartment and get more clothes for work.

"No."

The denial startled her. It wasn't actually the word, more the ferociousness with which he said it.

"I beg your pardon?" He wasn't her keeper and she certainly wasn't under arrest—at least not yet. He couldn't stop her from leaving.

"The only place you're safe right now is with me. Until this investigation is concluded that's where you're going to stay."

Fury shot from the tip of her toes to the roots of her hair. How dare he have sex with her and then act as if nothing had changed? "I think you've got that all wrong. Unless, of course, playing the part of bodyguard goes along with physical intimacy."

Her words were stinging, but true nonetheless.

He'd made a mistake in judgment. He couldn't change that, but he'd be damned if he'd admit that making love with her had been a mistake. It had simply been the wrong time and place. He braced his hands on the island's stone counter and leveled a gaze on her that he hoped conveyed the sincerity of his words. "It won't happen again."

Her eyes widened in anger, and when she would have responded with more furious words that revealed far more about the depth of hurt he'd inflicted, he added, "But not because I don't want it to, I do."

He gave her a moment to think about that, then continued, "I have a job to do. What happened between us wasn't part of the assignment. But I have to finish this job before I can allow any further personal involvement."

She blinked, clearly surprised by his frankness. "Then you don't regret that..."

Her words trailed off, but he knew what she was asking. "My only regret is about timing."

She nodded, her surprise morphing into confusion. "I'm not sure I understand completely, but..." She shrugged. "I guess I can live with that."

This was new ground for Simon. His emotions were too raw to analyze things beyond this point. The most important issue was focusing on the case and keeping Jolie safe.

He needed her to see that Boyer was a foe, not a friend, and she had to understand that this afternoon's event was no accident.

"We need to clarify a few things." He waited until she slid back onto the stool and gave him her full attention before continuing. "What happened on the street was no accident. I believe Brasco has already gotten word that you were *involved* in his son's death.''

''I didn't do it.'' She shook her head, the fear and uncertainty glittering in those wide green eyes once more. ''You have to believe that I didn't.'' She looked down at her hands and trembled. ''I couldn't.''

All that kept him from putting his arms around her and comforting her the way he wanted to was the island that stood between them. But he needed that distance, had to keep his perspective. Her safety was dependent upon his thinking straight. ''You don't have to convince me.'' Her gaze returned to his. ''But what I think, or whatever anyone else thinks, won't carry any weight with Brasco. He'll want revenge.''

''Are you sure it wasn't just an accident?''

Simon had gotten a brief but good look at the guy behind the wheel, as well as a fair description of the vehicle. He was quite sure. So sure, in fact, he'd put a call in to Johnson while Jolie showered. It would take him some time to narrow down the sketchy details, but Simon felt certain the driver would be connected to Brasco. The look on the guy's face had been one of determination. He'd known exactly what he was doing.

''I'm sure.'' The way she wilted beneath the weight of that reality only added to his misery. This was precisely why he never got involved on a personal level. It would be impossible for him to look at any of this objectively now.

''What am I supposed to do? If I go to the police...'' She fell silent again. She knew what that would involve.

This was the hard part for Simon. He had to convince her to carry on with her usual routine in hopes of forcing Brasco into making a move. Simon didn't even want to think about how risky that course of action was going to be, but it was the only way.

The only way to stop Brasco and ensure her continued safety.

"You do what you always do. You go to work and you do your job. The only difference is that you don't leave my sight."

She moistened her trembling lips and nodded. "Okay."

Simon wanted desperately to still those lips with his own, but that would only muddy the waters further. "I need you to tell me about your friend Erica." He'd already given her name to Johnson as a possible suspect. Admittedly, the connection was slim, but she did have black hair and she was close to Jolie. Close enough to know the kind of personal details necessary to carry off this level of setup.

"What do you want to know? She's my best friend." Jolie's expression turned guarded. "Why do you ask?"

Readying himself for battle, he gave her the unvarnished version. "Whoever is setting you up is close. Very close. He or *she* knows you well. Your comings and goings, your work routine, private details of your life. And—" he couldn't emphasize this part enough "—whoever it is has access. Access to you, to your home and your office. As far as I can see that boils down to two people, Boyer and your girlfriend Erica."

Hands on her hips, Jolie was off the stool, glaring at him with a mixture of disbelief and indignation in her eyes. "I can't believe you! First Mark, now Erica!" She cut a sharp left and started to pace the tiled floor. "We're best friends. She's the one who suggested I see a shrink and get hypnosis to try and figure out what happened that first night." Another glare arrowed Simon's way. "Why would she do that if she were trying to hurt me in some way?"

"I didn't say it was her, I said it had to be someone close to you."

Jolie threw up her arms in surrender. "Next you'll be accusing my father."

He'd actually considered that possibility, had Johnson looking into it as they spoke. Franklin Randolph had at one time run that very bank. And he had a secret that could easily have been used—still could be—as leverage against him. All of which made him vulnerable to a man like Brasco. Simon's hesitation obviously clued her in to his line of thinking.

"You can't be serious!" She paced back in his direction. "I won't talk about this." She moved her head firmly from side to side. "Don't bring my family and friends into this again." She marched straight up to him and jutted out her chin, looking him square in the eye. "I don't know what's going on! Maybe it is me." Emotion shimmered in those emerald depths. "Maybe I am crazy." The uncertainty turned to stone-cold determination. "But if you were half as good an investigator as you are a lover, you'd know that my father and friends don't have anything to do with this."

With that said she executed an about-face and stormed out of the room.

Leaving Simon to deal with just how right she was.

Chapter Twelve

Simon paid little attention to the presentation being offered by members of the audit team to the board of directors. Jolie hadn't looked his way even once since she'd entered her office at eight-thirty this morning. In fact, she hadn't spoken to him since before dinner last night. They'd argued and she'd walked away, refusing to discuss the subject any further.

He understood how she felt. Her life was being torn apart and she didn't know why. Whoever was behind the events had to be someone close to her, whether she wanted to admit it or not. Simon could see that, because he wasn't in her shoes. As much as he wanted to be wrong for her sake, he was very nearly certain he wasn't.

Johnson had found nothing on Jolie's friend Erica. She was clean—an advertising executive who'd risen above her foster home upbringing and made a very financially comfortable life for herself. Still, that didn't rule her out as far as Simon was concerned. He intended to check a few sources of his own.

There was still the situation with Renae, Jolie's assistant, as well. She insisted that a secretary from EastTrust had made the call summoning Jolie for Mr.

Knox. She'd failed to take a name and no one at EastTrust admitted to having made the call. Another dead end, just like Renae's background check. Clean. She still lived at home with her mother. The bank provided her sole income. No unexplainable accounts, deposits or withdrawals. Nothing. Mr. Knox had been at the dentist just as the secretary had said. And Jolie's father checked out as well, except for one long ago, slightly shady transaction, but it had nothing to do with business. His one transgression had been wholly personal and the only harm that could come from it was Jolie's learning the truth rather belatedly. Simon could tell her, but this was something that needed to come from her father.

"Don't you agree, Mr. Ruhl?"

The bank's president, Mr. Knox, waded into Simon's troubling thoughts, tugging him back to the presentation. All eyes were on him and all conversation had ceased. "Yes." Simon smiled. "I do agree." The hum of discussion restarted with a choreographed wave of nods.

Simon's cell phone, which he kept on silent, vibrated in his pocket. "Excuse me," he said to Mr. Knox as he rose from the table. "I have to take this."

As he exited the conference room Jolie looked up, but she quickly turned away when her gaze collided with his. Simon clenched his jaw and refused to be affected by her stubbornness. She'd see that he was right soon enough. He turned his back, leaned against the railing and looked out over the lobby as he flipped down the mouthpiece of his phone. "Simon Ruhl."

"Simon, it's Max."

Max was still on Grand Cayman Island. He

wouldn't bother to call unless he had news. "You have something new?"

As Max reported the results of his canvassing, Simon found himself holding his breath. He didn't want to hear what he feared Max was about to tell him.

"The captain made a positive ID." The sound of pages ruffling told Simon that he was flipping to a particular place in his notes. "He insisted the woman he took on the tour was the woman in the photograph, Jolie Randolph. The guy he described as accompanying her matches the description of Ray Brasco, Jr."

Denial hit Simon hard. He didn't want to know this, definitely didn't want to believe it. His gaze sought out Jolie, who was working diligently in her office. He couldn't be that wrong about her. Her innocence couldn't possibly be an act. He thought of the way she'd responded to his touch…to his kiss. That kind of response couldn't be faked, either. He was certain of it.

But what if he was wrong?

Could the woman he'd made love to last evening—the same one who'd felt so innocent and vulnerable in his arms—be a murderer?

"See if you can find someone who can back up the boat captain's ID. He may have been paid off. Check that avenue as well."

The silence on the other end of the line related loudly that Simon had said too much. Max had given him no reason to doubt the captain's word. There was no compelling motive to verify his testimony. Simon knew the drill, but this was different. As much as it pained him to admit it, what affected Jolie affected him on a very personal level.

"Will do," Max assured him. "The guy seems a little shady. It's possible he could have been bribed."

Max was exceedingly well trained. He'd worked with the Drug Enforcement Agency before joining the Colby Agency. Conducting a proper interrogation would be a simple matter for him. He'd had no reason to suspect a false statement or he would have mentioned that up front, but he rationalized Simon's request just to let him off the hook for overreacting.

"Thanks, Max. I owe you one."

Simon snapped the phone shut and dropped it back into his pocket. Someone was very thorough. But he would get to the bottom of it. Johnson had warned him again that he only had twenty-four hours. Simon hoped like hell that would be enough time to find something...anything to prove Jolie's innocence.

That last thought shook him. Since when had proving Jolie's innocence taken precedence over bringing down Brasco?

Shoving to the back of his mind the disturbing revelation he definitely did not want to analyze right now, he returned to the ongoing conference. He had a cover to keep in place. Until Brasco or his connection to Jolie made a move, Simon could only wait...and watch.

"MISS RANDOLPH."

Jolie looked up from the daily financial reports and summoned a smile. "Yes, Renae, come in."

Uneasiness slid through Jolie the moment she took a closer look at her assistant. She looked...puzzled or distressed somehow.

"Is something wrong?" She prayed there hadn't been another discrepancy in one of her accounts. That was the last thing she needed today. It was all she could do to maintain her composure as it was. She kept remembering the way the car had plowed toward her, seeing it from a whole different perspective now. And then there was the lovemaking with Simon.

Not to mention the argument and the fact that she wasn't speaking to him.

"A gentleman left a really strange message for you," Renae said hesitantly as she offered Jolie the slip of paper.

Fear charged through Jolie, stealing her breath as she read the words. *I know what you did.* No, it couldn't be from him...he was dead. Instantly her brain started to throb.

"Thank you," she managed to say past the lump of pure terror rising in her throat. She forced the corners of her lips to remain tilted upward. "Anything else?"

Renae shook her head and backed toward the door, her confusion no doubt complete now. "That's all."

Jolie waited until her assistant had left to look at the note again. Some fragile, diaphanous barrier burst inside her, freeing a savage emotion—something like sheer terror—that completely paralyzed her. The note fluttered from her grasp. She didn't really have to read it again. The words were seared across her irises as if she'd looked at the sun too long.

I know what you did.

It had to be from Brasco. Simon was right. He knew about her. Thought she was responsible for his son's death.

The phone on her desk rang, making her jump and sucking any remnants of air from her lungs.

Jolie blinked repeatedly and gulped in a breath.

Calm. She had to stay calm. Simon was right across the hall. Her gaze instantly shifted to confirm his presence. He'd said he would protect her. She had to trust that. It was all she had to hang on to. That and the belief that the people she considered to be her friends couldn't possibly be out to do her harm.

The phone rang again. This time she picked up the receiver. Renae was supposed to be holding her calls. When Jolie looked again she saw that the call had come in on her personal line. The one only those close to her knew about. Uncertainty contorted her stomach. Simon was making her paranoid. That's all. The only threat she had to worry about was Brasco.

And going to prison, a little voice reminded her. *Embezzlement. Murder.* She shuddered and banished the thoughts. She couldn't handle that right now.

"Jolie Randolph."

"Where in the world have you been, Jolie? I've been beside myself with worry."

Dad.

Relief flooded her, leaving her trembling with receding adrenaline.

"Dad." She searched for the right words. Simon had insisted that anything she told her father might endanger him. "I...I spent the night with a friend." She closed her eyes and prayed that he wouldn't push the matter.

"Anyone I know?" Jolie tensed. Her father chuckled. "I'm only teasing. You're way past having to report your whereabouts to your old man. But I was worried."

"Sorry." She moistened her lips and fought the urge to cry and tell him everything. The very idea that he might somehow be involved was beyond insane. He'd always been the perfect, loving father. "With the audit and everything it's just been crazy around here." That was the understatement of the millennium.

"Well, you know how I feel about you working so hard. Be sure you throw a little leisure time in there as well. I don't want anything to happen to my best girl. Stress can lead to all sorts of problems."

"Dad..." She knew before she spoke that he would refuse to talk about it. Though Simon was certain drugs had been the culprit in her blackouts and mental confusion, the past few days had driven home how easily her life could be devastated if she had indeed, inherited her mother's illness. "We've got to talk about Mom. I've been—"

"What happened to your mother has nothing to do with you, Jolie," he said sharply, uncharacteristically so. "How many times do I have to tell you that?"

Jolie hung her head and admitted defeat. She just didn't have it in her to fight with her dad today. "I'm sorry. I know you don't like to talk about Mom. Forgive me. We still on for Friday coffee?"

"Of course we are," he said in a more normal tone, though she could still hear the underlying frustration.

"Great. I'm glad you called." She grasped the phone more tightly, wishing he were here so she could hug him and feel the comfort of his familiar arms. "I love you, Dad."

"I love you, too, Jolie."

She hung up the receiver and automatically rubbed her bare left wrist. Damn, she hated that she'd lost that watch. Her father would definitely ask about it when he saw her again. She always, always wore it.

A quick rap on the door frame jerked her from her

worries. Mark lounged in the doorway, looking as smug and cocky as usual. "May I come in?"

How on earth could Simon think Mark had anything to do with any of this? He could be a pain in the neck, that was true, but a scheming criminal mastermind or worse? Jolie just couldn't see it.

She indicated one of the chairs facing her desk. "By all means. What's up?"

He strolled over to her desk, his hands buried in his trouser pockets. "Can't a guy stop in and say hello without a reason?" he asked, his tone teasing, but almost condescending. *Almost.*

Pushing down the impatience that boiled up at his tone, she made an inviting gesture. "Certainly. And how are you this morning?" She'd learned long ago that when Mark was in one of his catty moods it was best to just play along with him.

He propped one hip on the edge of her desk, which she found infinitely annoying—especially considering that he knew that particular posture irritated her.

"I missed seeing you this weekend. I hope you had a nice one."

Memories from the weekend flashed through her mind, reminding her of all that she wanted to forget. A chill sank clear to her bones. "It was fine," she lied, her voice so tight it fairly squeaked. Clearing her throat, she picked up a pen and toyed with it to occupy her hands. The urge to wring them was all but overpowering. What did he mean, he'd missed seeing her? They'd never socialized outside work.

"Well." He pushed to his feet. "I wouldn't want to keep you from your work."

"I'm sure you're busy as well," she offered, hoping to hasten him out the door.

He started to turn away, then hesitated and reached into his jacket pocket. "I almost forgot." He dangled something shiny in her face. "I thought you might have missed this. I know you rarely take it off."

The gold watch. Her watch. The one her father had given her for graduation. Mark dropped it onto her desk. "Don't worry, I took really good care of it for you."

"Where…where did you find it?" Her gaze moved up to meet his. The sinister look she saw there shocked her. She'd never seen him look like that before—so evil…threatening.

He leaned forward, bracing both hands on the desk in front of her, putting his face close to hers. "Don't you remember, Jolie?" he said cruelly. "You left it at my place the last time we were *together*."

She jerked her head from side to side. "What're you talking about?"

He smiled as he straightened away from her, but it wasn't pleasant. "I think you know what I'm talking about. Have a nice day," he called over his shoulder as he breezed out of her office.

She could only sit there and watch him walk away, horror inching up her rigid spine. When he was at last out of sight, she picked up her watch with numb fingers and stared at the delicate gold bracelet. There was only one way Mark could have gotten her watch.

He had to have taken it off her wrist while she lay unconscious next to a dead man.

BY MIDAFTERNOON Simon was pacing the conference room like a caged lion. Max hadn't called him back, which meant he hadn't found any evidence to refute the captain's positive ID of Jolie's picture. Simon told himself he didn't really need any additional evidence, that he trusted his instincts and his instincts told him that Jolie was innocent. But he was no fool. Well, at least not a complete fool. Being personally involved made a huge difference. He needed solid proof to refute *any* evidence against Jolie. Needed it for her sake as well as his own peace of mind.

The day had been one long meeting after another. The audit team was winding up its investigation, and Simon, in order to maintain his cover, was forced to sit in on each and every one. Thankfully, the conference room was in direct sight of Jolie. There would be two more meetings tomorrow and then it was done.

Another sign he was running out of time.

His gaze spanned the distance to where Jolie was conducting a meeting of her own with Boyer, Renae and a couple of other staff members.

Whatever Jolie wanted to believe, Simon was certain Boyer was responsible in whole or part for her troubles. Renae was pretty much in the clear, considering his last conversation with Johnson. The jury, however, was still out on Erica. A test could easily confirm if the hair found at the crime scene belonged to her, but for that they needed a warrant. And for a warrant they needed probable cause. Neither of which could be gotten as things stood.

As much as he despised admitting it, a definitive move on the part of one of the players was all that could salvage this case at the moment. There was only one downside. The move would involve Jolie's personal safety.

The bottom line twisted inside Simon like a knife. The image of Ray Brasco, Jr., lying in bed with a knife plunged to the hilt in his chest instantly formed in Simon's mind.

He didn't have to worry about a move. Somehow Brasco knew Jolie was involved. Johnson had confirmed that as well. The vehicle that had scarcely missed Jolie was registered to a man high on the food chain in Brasco's organization. High enough to be a right-hand man.

Brasco wanted his revenge on Jolie. Wanted it urgently enough to use his best. Simon had a bad feeling that yesterday's little display had only been the appetizer. The main event was coming.

For Jolie's sake, he had to be ready.

JOLIE TWIRLED the gold watch now safely clasped around her wrist. Simon had been right about Mark. Somehow he was involved in all this. She thought about the travel records, the transactions in the foreign bank. He could have done any or all of those things. All he'd needed was her access codes.

But how had he gotten them?

While she was drugged, maybe?

Was that why she had no recall of that weekend she'd supposedly spent traveling to Grand Cayman?

That's when it had all begun. The account had been set up. But then why wait all this time to make a move? It didn't make sense. Surely money laundering was something that had to be done on a regular basis. She sighed, disgusted. What did she know about money laundering? Nothing but what she'd learned in banking conferences, and that had only been the whitewashed version. This was real life. The down and dirty side.

Her gaze drifted to the conference room and the

man seated there in deep conversation on his cell phone. Simon wanted to help her. She really believed that. All the time she'd thought he suspected her, he was really watching out for her, it seemed.

He'd tried to tell her about Mark. She'd refused to believe. Now she knew the truth. Had his bitterness at missing out on the promotion run that deep? She massaged her forehead, allowing her fingertips to soothe the tension there. She'd wanted this promotion, but not at this cost. Her father had warned her, but she hadn't listened. She'd been willing to sacrifice any kind of personal life to obtain her goals. Look where it had gotten her.

The idea that Simon also suspected Erica ached like a wound being reopened. That just couldn't be. What on earth would Erica have to gain? They rarely discussed bank business. Erica was in advertising, for goodness sake.

No. Jolie refused to believe anyone other than Mark was involved. She couldn't be that naive.

Tears brimmed in her eyes and she had to grit her teeth to hold them back. She would not cry. She had to be strong now. She had to do something.

But what?

How could she help herself? Since she knew she'd been drugged and wasn't losing her mind, and now spent all her time with Simon, the journal was unnecessary. What else could she do? She knew nothing about the way a mob operation worked.

A stillness crept over her. No, she didn't know a thing about how to stop Brasco, but she did know how to stop Mark.

Anticipation burned through her veins. All she had to do was wait until he'd gone home for the day, and change his access codes. As his supervisor she could override his authority. Lock him out, so to speak. A smile stole over her lips. She could do that. If he was using her codes, or even his own, to launder money for Brasco, she would put an end to that.

Then she'd get a reaction out of him. She chewed her lower lip thoughtfully. It was a given that she couldn't tell Simon. He wouldn't go for it. He'd say it was too dangerous. Not to mention she wasn't ready to admit that he was right about Mark. She had to see for herself…to know for sure, first. So she wouldn't tell Simon. If she cut off Mark's access he'd have to do something, make some move—if, in fact, he was as guilty as it now seemed he was.

Maybe he'd even confess to what he'd been up to in lieu of facing Brasco's wrath. She wondered what a man like Brasco would do if his means of accomplishing his goal was stopped.

One thing was certain. By this time tomorrow, she would know.

Chapter Thirteen

Simon opened the passenger door of his SUV and waited for Jolie to gather her purse and briefcase before she emerged into the humid morning air. The dank smell of the bank's basement parking garage added another layer of uneasiness to Simon's already mounting tension. He surveyed the area again as he waited. Every instinct warned him that something wasn't right, but he couldn't fully trust his instincts any longer.

In spite of his best efforts, his emotions were ruling him. He swore under his breath. Jolie had refused to speak to him or even to eat with him last night. He'd attempted to make her understand that he had his reasons for his suspicions regarding her friends, but she wasn't interested in hearing what he had to say.

She'd gone to bed early, leaving him to stew in a cauldron of uncertainty and worry of his own making. The only thing that kept him from calling Victoria and admitting that he'd lost his perspective on this case was the fear that she would immediately send a replacement to relieve him of duty. Simon couldn't protect Jolie if he wasn't on the case.

A sigh hissed past his lips. The need to have his

vengeance where Brasco was concerned was still there; he owed the memory of his partner that much. But that need had taken a back seat to his obsession with Jolie.

Obsession. Simon shook his head. Nothing in his past had prepared him for this situation. Not his privileged childhood or his Ivy League education or even his intensive training and experience as a federal agent and then a Colby Agency investigator. The reputation he'd garnered for calm, reserve, for having a level head in the worst case scenario since signing on with the Colby Agency, was now shot to hell. He was at a complete loss to explain how this woman had affected him so deeply.

Every step, every action was hindered by thoughts of her.

Jolie settled high heeled, strappy leather sandals onto the concrete floor and pushed up from her seat, coming face-to-face with him and unconsciously trapping herself in the V made by the open car door and his body. He reacted instantly, his muscles going taut. A spiral of need tightened his abdomen, sending a rush of desire straight to his loins.

When she would have slid between him and the door, he braced his arm atop it and moved in closer. His instincts were buzzing. Something was up. He had to make sure she understood just how precarious the situation was. ''I need some sense that you're taking this seriously.''

She tilted her head back and glared at him, those green eyes shooting daggers at him. ''I'm not stupid, Simon. I am taking this seriously. I understand that someone tried to kill me. What else do you want from me? I'm with you twenty-four hours a day. You're controlling every move I make.''

She focused that furious gaze on his tie then, refusing to maintain eye contact. That she wouldn't look at him as he spoke to her only frustrated him more.

"I'm referring to the part about Boyer..." She shifted when he mentioned the man's name. The move was subtle, but there was a definite new tension in her posture. She was apparently still in denial regarding her friends. "You have to know that he represents a threat. You can't trust anyone right now."

She looked up at him then, her eyes openly accusing. "And what about you, Simon? Can I trust you?"

A glimmer of vulnerability escaped her stern demeanor. She was scared. He could feel the fear radiating from her. He wanted to touch her, to reassure her, but she didn't want that. "You can trust me. The only thing that matters to me right now is protecting you." There. He'd said it out loud. And it was true. As much as he wanted to take down Brasco, he wanted to protect Jolie more. Whatever that made him, he was helpless to change it.

She swallowed tightly. He watched the movement of delicate muscle along the column of her throat. She searched his eyes and then his face for what felt like an eternity before she responded to his soul-baring confession. "Don't let me down, Simon," she urged, her voice thick with emotion. "I don't think I can take another betrayal."

He leaned closer, desperate to somehow make her believe in him despite the many reasons he'd given her not to. "I won't let you down," he murmured, his lips brushing her temple. She shivered and his entire physical being reacted. He lowered his mouth toward hers and she instinctively lifted those lush lips to meet his. The kiss was brief but potent. More intense than anything he'd ever experienced and yet easy and unhurried somehow. It was a kiss that spoke of mutual trust...of mutual need, with an underlying desperation that rendered them both completely vulnerable.

When he drew back just a little her eyes were still closed, and he knew for a certainty then that he'd gained her full trust. For the first time in his life he feared failure. He couldn't let that happen. He set his jaw firmly. He wouldn't let it happen.

"Wait," she whispered, her eyes still closed tightly.

He remained perfectly still, his face only inches from hers.

"I want this to last just a little longer."

He couldn't help himself. He had to take her into his arms. She didn't resist. There, in the massive, deserted parking garage, he held her that way, close to his heart, until she was ready to face the uncertainty of the day.

JOLIE WENT ABOUT BUSINESS as usual as the morning progressed. As tough as it proved, she did a pretty fair job of keeping her mind on work. She'd suffered a tension-filled, restless night, what with avoiding Simon, refusing to talk to him, and then the nightmares. But she'd had to keep her distance. Otherwise she might have lost her resolve and told him what she'd done. She hated the idea that she'd lied to him about finding the watch, but she needed to see her plan through. This morning, thankfully, all had been quiet, giving her a much-needed respite, until late afternoon.

Mark entered her office then without even knocking—her first clue that he was upset. One look at his expression told her he was way beyond upset. She didn't need to ask to know that he'd tried to access the system she'd locked him out of.

"Good morning, Mark," she said casually, scarcely sparing him a glance for fear he'd see the truth in her eyes.

"Is IBS down?" he demanded, his tone just a fraction shy of hysterical.

Was something about this day of the week or the month special? she wondered. Could she have accidentally picked the perfect day for rendering him impotent? That would be just too perfect.

"No, it's not down," she assured him, her tone surprisingly calm. "You know that system never goes down."

He flared his hands, his agitation mounting visibly. "Then what's the problem? It won't let me in."

Jolie leaned back in her chair, uncertain where this was going. Could Simon be more right about Mark than she'd realized? "You're locked out because the audit team is doing one last system check." She angled her head inquisitively, searching the face of the man she'd called a friend for as long as she'd been employed at this bank. "Do you have a problem with that? It's only for the day."

"Are you crazy? Of course I have a problem with that!" he fairly shouted. "This is a bank, damn it. How can I conduct business for my clients if I can't access the system? What am I supposed to tell them?" Fury flashed in his eyes. His distress had mushroomed into outright rage. "What the hell is going on here, Jolie?" His hands went to his hips and he glared down at her with more hostility than she'd believed he possessed.

She tensed, but fought to keep up the facade of calm. *Breathe.* Just breathe. Stay calm. She had to play this out. "Bring your transactions to me and I'll take care of them personally. I'm sorry I didn't mention this yesterday. But don't worry, for today I'll take care of anything you need."

"Why am I locked out and you're not?" He was literally seething now. His fists were clenched and he looked ready to lunge at someone. Jolie's tension escalated to a higher level. Maybe this hadn't been such a bright idea. But she had to know.

This just wasn't the answer she'd hoped for.

Jolie hoped Simon wasn't watching, but she was sure he would be. He might burst through the door behind Mark any moment. That would ruin everything. She had to be sure about Mark. She couldn't go through another day not knowing. His agitation thus far could still be chalked up to peer rivalry. He hadn't really crossed any kind of line yet.

"Because I'm the head of the department," she said evenly. "Don't take it personally. Just bring me your transactions and everything will be fine."

For one long beat she thought that was going to be the end of it. Hope bloomed inside her. Maybe Simon was wrong. Then something changed in Mark's eyes. Pure evil rose to the surface, banishing all signs of distress or fear. "I know what you're up to," he accused, his voice soft now, but more threatening than if he'd been ranting at her like before. "But it won't work. You don't know what you're up against. You can't stop them.''

She shrugged, somehow managing a look of confusion despite the fear banding around her chest. He wanted her scared, and she couldn't let him see that he'd succeeded. "I can't imagine what you mean, Mark. Are you sure you're all right? You look a little shaky. Maybe you need a day off." The memory of him telling her that she needed a few days off echoed in her brain, the unintentional jab adding even more impact to her words.

He took a step in her direction, his glare so thoroughly filled with hate now that she had to fight the urge to run. Her fingers clenched around her chair arms to keep her anchored there. "One hour," he said tightly. "You have one hour to let me back in. If you don't, you'll be sorry." He looked at the clock on the wall for emphasis, ensuring that she took note of the time, 1:00 p.m. Then he added, "One hour, Jolie."

The moment he'd left her office the courage she'd displayed scattered like dust in the wind. Her heart pounded even faster and her palms grew damp with perspiration.

She'd done it.

Her gaze went of its own volition to the clock. One hour. He'd said one hour. Could she face the consequences of her bold move alone?

She searched the crowd of faces in the conference room across the corridor for Simon's. He looked right at her, his expression questioning. She knew instantly that he'd watched the exchange between her and Mark and wondered if everything was all right. Then and there the final decision was made. She couldn't give him even the slightest indication that anything was wrong, so she smiled. He smiled back. She quickly shifted her attention to the files on her desk. In her present state, if he got too close, she might just break down and tell him what she'd done. He would only get in the way in his attempts to protect her. She needed those glass walls between them. She had to do this. Had to be strong. Special Agent Johnson had warned Simon that he would have to bring her in no later than five o'clock today. She had no proof that she was innocent of the murder someone—Mark maybe, though as shocked as she was to learn he was somehow involved, she still couldn't see him as a cold-blooded killer—had attempted to pin on her.

Her word that Mark was, indeed, involved wouldn't be enough. She needed tangible proof that he was the one dealing with the mob. At least then there would be a connection between him and the murder. Jolie felt certain that if the police had something on him, he would cave under intense questioning. He would never hold out if he thought spilling his guts would save him. Whether he'd killed that man or not, he had to know something about it. Otherwise he wouldn't have had her wristwatch in his possession.

He was the key. She was certain of it. Mark could clear her. She'd forced him into a corner. If he was scared enough, he'd make a desperate move. She was positive.

All she had to do was wait. She looked at the clock again. And prayed she'd done the right thing.

BY TWO O'CLOCK THE LAST of the audit meetings had broken for a late lunch. Simon stood and exchanged the expected pleasantries with various members of the board, but his full attention never left Jolie.

She'd remained in her office all morning except for one quick trip to the ladies' room. The only time he'd had cause to grow anxious was when Boyer had swaggered through her door. Though Simon couldn't see the man's face as the conversation developed, his posture gave Simon reason to believe that he hadn't been a happy camper. Just when Simon had been certain he would need to intervene, Boyer had left, visibly more agitated than when he'd arrived. Jolie's forced smile hadn't given Simon much of a reason to relax his guarded stance, but it had kept him from abruptly walking out of his meeting.

He had just three hours left before having to meet Johnson for the required statement from Jolie, but his cover at the bank was still necessary. Monitoring Boyer's activities remained the best shot at taking down Brasco. Not to mention that Boyer might just be Jolie's only way clear of suspicion.

Though Simon had tried to prepare her for the upcoming meeting with Johnson, between her refusal to talk to him and the tension building inside him, warning of some imminent danger, Simon couldn't be sure he'd gotten through to her. His emotions were too jumbled to cast a firm impression. The only good thing that had come of any of this so far was that Johnson had been able to keep Medford off Simon's back.

His cellular phone vibrated and he quickly retrieved it from his pocket. Not until he saw the number on the caller ID did he remember that he hadn't heard from Max in nearly twenty-four hours. He an-

swered before the second ring, a new kind of anticipation mounting inside him.

"I've got what we've been looking for." Max
sounded hyped. He didn't wait for Simon to reply.
"The captain works for Brasco. One of his former
lady friends told me he'd bragged to her about es-
corting a big league mob boss from Atlanta whenever
he was in town. She couldn't remember his name, but
she did remember his son."

"Good work, Max." A surge of relief reeled
through Simon. No one had positively ID'd Jolie as
the woman who'd set up the account. That didn't precisely clear her, but it helped. No wonder he hadn't
heard from Max in so long—he'd been too busy woo-
ing information. Simon definitely owed him one.

"There's more," Max added breathlessly. "You
know the black hair you mentioned that was found at
the crime scene?"

"What about it?"

"My informant also told me that the son often
brought a female companion to the island with him.
Guess what color her hair was?"

Anticipation shot through Simon. "I'm going to
fax another photo to your hotel. Find out if the
woman in the picture was the companion."

"Will do."

Simon ended the call and immediately punched in
Johnson's number. "I need another favor."

"I hate to tell you this, friend, but you've about
reached your maximum credit line."

Simon didn't doubt for a moment that he was serious, but forged ahead just the same. "Jolie's friend
Erica Thurston. Can you pull a photo from DMV or
some other source?"

The sound of shuffling papers rustled over the line. "I can do you one better than that. I've got her photo already from her firm's Website. One of my guys found it during the routine background search."

Perfect. "Fax it to my partner." Simon rattled off the number. "One thing more," he added when Johnson would have disconnected. "Can you have one of your techs do a little electronic makeover and give her blond hair and green eyes?"

"Hmm." Johnson paused thoughtfully. "I see where you're going with this, I just don't know why."

"Trust me," Simon urged. "I'll fill you in at five."

"All right," Johnson agreed. "Don't be late."

Simon put his phone away and decided it was past time that Jolie took a break. There was a lounge in the bank. Lunch could be delivered. He didn't want her out in the open any more than absolutely necessary.

As he stepped from the conference room, Boyer rushed past him. Briefcase in hand, the guy didn't look up once as he seemingly fled the bank. The uneasy feeling that had been nagging at Simon all day nudged him now. Boyer was up to something. Johnson had a man tailing him at Simon's urging, so whatever he had on his agenda the feds would be privy to.

When Simon turned his attention back to Jolie she was still staring after Boyer, worry etched across her face. Did she know something about his hasty exit? Simon shook off that thought. Jolie had no part in this. Maybe she was concerned because of something Boyer had said this morning. That was the most likely scenario. There was only one way to find out.

Simon crossed the corridor and stuck his head inside her office. "How about a lunch break?"

She started and swung her attention to him. "I'm sorry...what was that?"

"Lunch," he urged. "I know you eat. It's time." He tapped his watch. She reacted to the move as if he'd thrown something at her.

She shook her head, and before he could argue, she threw out a flimsy excuse. "I'm too busy. You go ahead. I'm not even hungry."

Like he was going to do that. "Jolie—"

"Oh, Simon!" a voice called.

He shifted his focus to the corridor, where Mr. Knox, followed by a half-dozen of the board members, marched toward him. Simon stifled his impatience and worked up a smile. "Surely you're not reconvening already, gentlemen." He hoped like hell they weren't. He needed time to update Jolie. To make sure she was all right.

Mr. Knox exchanged a perfunctory greeting with Jolie, then turned back to Simon. "Actually, we hoped we could clear up one other small matter."

What the hell. "Of course." Simon led the way back into the conference room. He glanced back at Jolie once more and did a double take. She was staring in the direction Boyer had disappeared. But that wasn't what disturbed Simon. What bothered him was the worry still claiming her expression.

Something had gone down between those two.

He turned his attention back to the men grouped around the conference table. As soon as he could get rid of these guys he intended to find out exactly what had happened.

Jolie forced her eyes to stay on the pages scattered

on her desk. She had to think about something else besides Mark's abrupt departure. He'd walked out with his briefcase. She supposed he could have a meeting, but she had a terrible feeling that it was something far worse than that.

What would Brasco do to Mark if he couldn't perform his usual service? She flinched at the thought that she might have inadvertently sentenced her colleague to death. She closed her eyes and exhaled sharply.

God, what had she done?

She needed to tell Simon. He would know what to do. Whatever Mark had done to her, she couldn't let him go off like this. How could she live with herself if she did nothing?

Jolie stood. She couldn't let this thing she'd set in motion go any further.

"Miss Randolph, you have a customer."

Jolie looked up to find Renae standing at her door, a tall man wearing a dark gray business suit behind her.

"Oh." She tried to recall the man's name but couldn't. She was pretty sure she hadn't met him before. "Please, come in."

Renae stepped aside for the man to enter Jolie's office. "Miss Randolph will take good care of you, Mr. Nelson."

Good old Renae. She could always be counted on for a last minute save.

"Have a seat, Mr. Nelson." Jolie smiled widely. She assumed that Renae had brought this customer to her since Mark was unavailable. Another stab of guilt tore through her.

"That won't be necessary, Miss Randolph." The

man stood between her desk and the chair she'd offered. "This wouldn't be a good place for us to have our discussion."

She frowned, puzzled. "I'm not sure I understand. Did you want to set up a new account or have you been working with Mr. Boyer already?"

The man smiled, but it did nothing to lend pleasantness to his face. His features were granite hard and every bit as cold. His eyes were too small for his face and his hawklike nose tried valiantly to make up for the lack of balance.

"I've worked with Mr. Boyer for quite some time, but that seems to be about to change."

Fear streaked through Jolie. The man's smile widened to a grin when he saw the recognition in her eyes.

"You'll need to come with me, Miss Randolph."

She swung her head from side to side. "I'm very busy. I can't—"

The man came around the side of her desk. Her heart stalled midbeat and shuddered in her chest. He leaned down as if looking at something on her desk. "You feel this?" He grabbed her hand and rubbed it against the hard steel weapon hidden within his jacket pocket. "I don't want to have to use it. But don't think I won't." His grip on her wrist turned punishing. "Now come with me or your friend Boyer is a dead man." His gaze connected with hers, sending another chill through her with those stone-cold gray eyes. "That's a Glock 9 mm you felt in there. Fifteen rounds plus one in the chamber. How many of those fine gentlemen over there in the conference room do you think I could take out before your pathetic excuse for security guards stopped me?"

A tiny gasp escaped her before she could stop it.

The evil man nodded. "Any of 'em friends of yours?"

She didn't have to answer. He knew. He knew by the horror that gripped her heart like a vise and erupted into panic on her face. She thought of Simon and Mr. Knox. Of Henry, the security guard on duty, and his granddaughter who depended on him.

"Then you be a good little girl and come with me." The man stepped back. "Ladies first," he said, taking the opportunity to leer at her.

Her body numb, her feet clumsy, Jolie rounded her desk and led the way out of her office. She peered into the conference room the entire time, praying that Simon would look her way, but Mr. Knox and two of the other men blocked his view.

"Speed it up, Miss Randolph." The man moved up behind her, ushering her forward with his big body. "We don't want anyone in the bank to have to die."

Her fingers ice cold, she grasped the railing and descended the stairs down to the gallery. She smiled when customers greeted her, but the reaction was so ingrained it was more autonomic than conscious. She didn't want anyone hurt. But she didn't want to die, either.

Mere feet from the massive front entrance, she hesitated despite the man's insistence that she keep moving. She took one last look up at the conference room. Her heart pounded in a frantic rhythm when Simon's gaze met hers. She prayed he would read the message she tried to relay with just a look.

Help me.

Chapter Fourteen

Simon burst through the double entry doors onto the crowded sidewalk. Frantic to spot Jolie, he scanned face after face.

Damn it. Where was she?

He looked for the tall gray-haired guy in the charcoal suit, but he was nowhere to be seen.

Defeat pounded in Simon's chest. She hadn't taken her purse with her. No way to track her.

He'd lost her.

Brasco.

The son of a bitch.

He had her.

Simon reached for his cell phone. It vibrated in his palm. Johnson's cellular number flashed across the tiny screen. Simon snatched it open. ''Brasco's got Jolie,'' he said in a rush, already running toward the underground garage and his car. ''One of his men just left the bank with her.''

''He's probably on his way to the warehouse,'' Johnson said grimly. ''There's something going down. My man followed Boyer there. Five minutes later Brasco arrived.''

Fear slammed into Simon's gut. "Give me the address."

He was already barreling out of his parking slot as Johnson recited the directions to the warehouse.

"We'll wait for you if we can," Johnson assured him.

Simon squealed out onto the street, causing a chorus of honking from a dozen startled drivers. "Don't let anything happen to her."

"You know her chances aren't good. Once she's inside that warehouse with Brasco—"

"Then stop the bastard before he takes her inside," Simon roared as he swerved from lane to lane to get around slow-moving traffic.

"You know we can't jeopardize the whole operation for one person."

Simon didn't bother to argue, just threw the phone across the seat and focused on driving. He had to move faster. Though he knew Johnson would be conscious of safety as much as possible, most of those in the line of fire between the feds and Brasco were deemed expendable. Jolie would be right smack in the middle.

"DO YOU KNOW who I am?"

At the sound of the man's voice, Jolie stopped struggling against the unyielding hands holding her. She looked up and drew in a harsh breath. Though the man was older, his hair gray and thinning, his eyes were eerily familiar.

"The man you murdered was my son," he said, his tone savage, his eyes glinting with hatred.

She shook her head. "No. I didn't kill him. It was a setup. I—"

"Save your excuses! I know what you did."

Her heart stumbled before jolting into an even faster rhythm. She was going to die. "I swear—"

"Silence!"

The solitary word echoed through the looming warehouse. No one moved or spoke while he stood there glowering down at her, as if he could cause her death simply by sheer force of will. Jolie didn't doubt for a moment that he could.

She had no idea how long she'd been here. It felt like hours but could have been mere minutes. A dozen or more of his men loitered about, all armed and dangerous looking. She had no hope of escaping even if the brute manhandling her were to loosen his grip for some reason. Simon would never find her.

Simon.

She didn't want him to find her, she thought frantically. There was no way he could fight off all these men. *Please,* she prayed, *don't let him come.* Tears welled in her eyes. She didn't want him to die, too. She struggled to remember the last thing she'd said to him and to her father. Had she told her father she loved him? Had Simon read in her eyes just how much she cared for him?

Brasco moved closer to her, his girth making his breath harsh even with that small effort. "Very shortly, Miss Jolie Randolph, you will die."

She trembled, but quickly caught herself. She would not give this evil man the satisfaction of seeing her fear. "Do what you have to," she told him, her tone so flat and emotionless she was startled that it came from her. "But you'll be killing an innocent woman."

He made a sound that wasn't quite a laugh. "You

would already be dead if not for the ineptness of my former associate.''

The man who'd tried to run her over, she realized. His failure had cost him his life. Nausea churned in Jolie's stomach. This was like a nightmare from a bad movie. Too horrible to be real. She looked from one menacing face to the next. But it was real. Her pulse tripped into overdrive. Vaguely she regretted that she would spend her final moments of life in the presence of these goons.

''I've always known that if you wanted something done right you had to do it yourself.'' Brasco leaned closer, his putrid breath making her shudder. ''But before you die I will have my money.''

His sudden change of subject startled her, dragged her full attention back to him alone. She shuddered again at the murderous look in his eyes. ''What money?''

''On dates of my choosing a sum of money is transferred through a number of accounts, eventually ending up in a very special account, also of my choosing. This money is of utmost importance to me. Today that didn't happen, and I understand that you're the reason it didn't.''

She'd been right in her earlier assumption. Mark had had a job to do and he'd failed. The realization that the other man who'd failed Brasco was dead burst inside her like shattering glass.

''Where's Mark?'' she demanded, her voice stronger than it had a right to be.

Brasco gestured to one of the men across the room. He disappeared into the shadows for a moment, but quickly returned with Mark in tow.

Jolie's breath caught when she saw what they'd

done to him. They'd beaten him within an inch of his life. His face was swollen and bloody. She'd caused this. She couldn't help the sting of guilt. Whatever he'd done to her, she shouldn't have put him in this position. She closed her eyes, barely stemming the flow of tears. Why was this happening to her? How had Mark gotten himself into something like this?

Brasco snapped his fingers and another of his men came forward. He placed a laptop computer on a nearby crate and connected a line from a cellular phone.

"Now." Brasco turned to her. "You will make the transfer and perhaps prolong your friend's life for a few moments more."

"Do it, Jolie," Mark cried hoarsely. "He'll kill both of us if you don't."

He would kill them both, anyway. She was certain of that.

She turned to Brasco and looked him straight in the eye and lied. "I can't. I have to be inside the bank to make that kind of transfer."

Mark howled in agony. "Just do it!" he screamed.

Brasco lifted a skeptical eyebrow. "Your friend seems to think otherwise."

Every nerve in her body pulsed with fear. Was she doing the right thing? If she put him off, maybe he wouldn't kill them right away. Maybe the FBI would come to the rescue. Simon would surely call his friend Agent Johnson. He'd said he didn't want her out of his sight. He had to be looking for her…but then he'd be in danger, too.

Brasco nodded once and a hissing pop rent the air.

Mark crumpled to the dirty concrete floor.

Jolie cried out and would have gone to help him

had the brute behind her not manacled her arms once more.

"I'll ask you one last time," Brasco said quietly. "Give me my money."

A new kind of numbness—shock, she recognized in some remote place in her brain—tugged Jolie toward the darkness. The feeling was familiar. She was going to faint. But she couldn't. She had to...

"Do it!" Brasco roared.

He could kill her, but he would never get his hands on that money.

She looked straight into his eyes. "No."

Another nod from Brasco and the man holding her yanked her head back. A cold steel blade suddenly pressed against her throat. Her heart crashed against her rib cage, threatening to burst from her chest. She'd gambled and lost. Brasco was going to kill her, anyway.

"Freeze!"

The command came from somewhere in the shadows near the front of the warehouse.

Everything lapsed into slow motion then. Gunfire erupted. Flashes of light lit up the dark areas of the warehouse. Brasco's men were scrambling for cover. The blade bit into her flesh. She cried out and felt the warm blood bloom, then ooze down her skin. She was going to die. Darkness threatened again as the room started to spin around her.

The man holding Jolie shoved her to her knees and dragged her behind the crate. He cowered behind her. "Make the transfer," he snarled close to her ear.

When she didn't respond, he jerked her hard by the hair, wrenching a yelp from her. "Do it!"

She felt the prick of the knife as he jabbed it into

her side. She fumbled for the keyboard of the laptop, wondering if a stray bullet would strike her and end this horror now.

Her mind went completely blank and her fingers fell limp on the keys. She waited helplessly for the slice of the knife to plunge into her flesh.

The man suddenly slumped to one side. She stared down at him, her eyes noting the strange hole in the middle of his forehead, but her brain didn't register right away what it meant. The knife lay on the floor, too, no longer poised to end her life. She frowned, trying to think how that had happened.

Then she was in Simon's arms. She wasn't sure how she got there but she wept against his broad chest, praying that this part was real and that she wasn't dreaming.

"It's all right now. Brasco is dead. He can't hurt anyone anymore."

"Mark..." she murmured, and turned to where his motionless body lay.

"Was Brasco's connection at the bank. He was trying to set you up, Jolie. To get your position, probably."

She shook her head, still finding it hard to believe that she'd been so wrong about him.

"Damn." Simon turned her around and looked more closely at her throat. "You need a paramedic."

He pulled her through the chaos toward the front of the building. Somehow her feet kept up with his long strides. It all felt so surreal now. Bodies were everywhere. Federal agents were arresting those who weren't dead. The laptop was being confiscated. It looked to Jolie like a war zone, and she belatedly realized that it was. And the good guys had won. She was alive.

Simon ushered her to a waiting ambulance. She didn't bother asking why there were several here. She supposed they had anticipated injuries and casualties. Then she saw a couple of downed agents being provided with medical attention, and it all coalesced.

A paramedic immediately settled her onto a cot in the rear of an ambulance and went to work on her injuries. She had to remove her jacket and loosen her blouse to give him access to her side.

"Just flesh wounds, ma'am," he assured her. "You'll be fine."

She nodded. She wanted to smile in gratitude, but her lips wouldn't make the transition.

"Simon!"

A man slightly older than Simon, wearing some sort of protective vest and a cap with FBI emblazoned across it, raced over to where Simon stood next to the vehicle's open doors. She hadn't noticed until then that Simon wore a vest, too.

"We got him!" The man clapped Simon on the back. "It's about time."

Simon nodded, looking more weary than Jolie had ever seen him. He didn't take his eyes off her. The idea that his weariness had something to do with concern for her made her feel giddy. Or maybe it was the shock returning.

"This is Special Agent Johnson," Simon explained, drawing her into the conversation.

"Miss Randolph, we're glad you made it out in one piece." The man's smile was genuine. "We're also very glad that we didn't have to pursue charges against you. I'll still need that statement regarding the events of this past weekend, but that can wait.''

The FBI had thought she was involved in all this. Thank God that was over. ''I don't remember much about that night,'' she told him. ''I don't know if I'll be much help.''

''Whatever you can give us will be helpful, I'm sure.'' He shook his head. ''We were definitely wrong about you all the way around.''

The sting of the antiseptic made her flinch, but it was Johnson's words that snapped her to full attention.

He nodded in emphasis. ''Simon and I were both convinced that you were the key to Brasco's operation at the bank. We knew Boyer was involved, but we were certain you were the primary.''

A new kind of shock radiated through her. Her gaze swung to Simon. He'd thought she was a suspect. She'd believed that at first, but then... That's why he'd been there at every turn, had kept after her, seducing her with that dark, alluring charm. Watching her every move. He'd lied to her...told her it was Mark he suspected.

Simon glanced away from the accusation in her eyes, and that spoke volumes about his guilt.

Johnson looked from one to the other, suddenly uncomfortable. ''But that's all cleared up now,'' he interjected. ''The moment Boyer left the bank today and came to this warehouse we knew it was him.''

Had Simon suspected her until today? Even while they'd made love? She pushed the paramedic's hand away. ''I'd like to go now, if that's all right with you, Agent Johnson.''

There was no way to miss the fury in her tone.

"Well—"

Simon cut off anything he would have said. "I don't want you alone right now. There are still loose ends to tie up on this case."

She looked at him with all the disgust she could manage. "I wasn't asking *your* permission."

"I'll have one of my men take you home and stay with you," Johnson suggested placatingly, his face red with embarrassment that he'd so obviously put his foot in his mouth.

"Fine." Jolie climbed out of the ambulance. "I'd like to go right now."

Johnson nodded. "I'll take care of it." He hurried over to one of his men, probably relieved to escape the thickening tension.

"Let me explain," Simon urged, stepping into her path.

"No way." She blinked back the rush of tears. Damn it. She would not cry right now. She'd been manhandled, jabbed and sliced with a knife, and almost killed. She wasn't going to cry now after surviving all that. She should be happy. She should be damned ecstatic.

"Jolie." He stopped her with a hand on her arm when she would have walked away. Despite her fury, a zing of electricity accompanied his touch. Damn her foolish heart, as well.

She retreated from his touch. "I don't ever want to see you again. Go back to Chicago." She walked away without looking back. It was over.

It was *all* over.

On the way to her apartment the agent assigned to stay with her until further notice talked nonstop. Jolie resisted the impulse to put her hands over her ears.

She didn't want to hear any of it. Especially the parts about Simon.

"He was one of the best agents we'd ever had." He shook his head. "But after Brasco killed his partner, he just walked away...gave it all up. I guess that's why he was so determined to break this case. He wasn't going back to Chicago until he'd gotten Brasco. Man, that's some kind of loyalty."

No wonder Simon had been willing to do whatever it took to solve this case, even sleep with her. He had a personal motive—vengeance.

Jolie closed her eyes and shut out the rest of the agent's words. None of it had been real. Mark had used her, even tried to have her charged with murder just to get her job. Simon had used her, as well...to get to Mark and Brasco.

Simon had been right about one thing. She couldn't trust anyone.

Later, after a shower and a couple of glasses of wine, Jolie curled up on her sofa in a comfortable pair of jeans and her favorite T-shirt. The agent guarding her apartment chose to do so outside her front door. She supposed his decision had had something to do with her icy demeanor. She needed to be alone. To think. To lick her emotional wounds.

She closed her eyes and tried to banish the images and the hurt. Why in the world did she have to go falling in love with a guy who couldn't love her back?

She sighed. Damn. It was true. She did love him. The look on his face when Johnson had spilled the truth was nearly convincing; he sincerely hated that the words had hurt her. But she refused to be fooled again. What difference did any of it make? He would be going back to Chicago, anyway.

A knock on her door dragged her from the troubling thoughts. She huffed an exasperated breath. Mr. Talks-A-Lot probably needed to use the facilities. She'd made him a pot of coffee, so she supposed she had no one to blame there but herself.

She opened the door and he flashed a smile. "There's someone here to see you, Miss Randolph. She says she's a friend of yours, but my orders—"

"Jolie, are you all right?" Erica pushed past the guy and threw her arms around her.

Jolie sagged into her friend's embrace. And for the second time today she wept.

Once Jolie had assured the agent that Erica was okay, her friend guided her back inside and to the sofa. "Tell me what happened." She poured Jolie another glass of wine and thrust it into her hand. "I called the bank to chat with you and Renae said something awful was going on."

Slowly, between crying jags, Jolie told Erica about Mark and Brasco and the money laundering. Finally she culminated the story with a patchy version of this evening's events.

"I can't believe I didn't see through Mark." She leaned back against the sofa and closed her eyes in defeat. "And Simon. How could I have fallen in love with a guy who thought I was a criminal?"

Erica patted her hand. "These things do happen."

Jolie's eyes snapped open in remembered horror. "God, I forgot to tell you. Mark is dead." She blinked back renewed tears. "One of Brasco's men shot him right in front of me."

"I know."

The words took a moment to penetrate the comfortable haze the wine had formed around Jolie's emotions. *Erica knew*. That was…impossible. Jolie blinked and shifted her gaze to her friend, intending to ask if the people at the bank had somehow already heard the news. The haze evaporated instantly at the sight of the gun in Erica's hand.

"Let's make this as painless as possible, shall we?" Erica smiled facetiously. "We'll go to the bank and you'll transfer the funds and maybe I'll let you live."

"No." The word was heavy with hurt. Jolie shook her head, refusing to believe. How could everyone she cared about betray her?

Erica nodded. "Afraid so. Now, let's get moving. I have a plane to catch."

"I don't understand," Jolie said, her voice quavering. This was just too much.

"You weren't supposed to get that promotion." She sighed. "But Mark just wasn't good enough at times. But you see," she continued, clearly proud of herself, "I always have a backup plan. That's why I befriended you. If anything ever happened to Mark, I'd have you." Her smile turned petulant. "But the old man didn't like that Mark had to work his business dealings around you. It made things riskier, more complicated. So Mark and I devised a way to get rid of you and make ourselves a little nest egg in the process. Only every time we drugged you hoping you'd get yourself killed, you somehow survived. Then you told me about waking up in that strange bed and new inspiration struck."

Jolie shook her head. "I don't want to hear this."

Erica jabbed her with the gun. "Get up. You're going to hear it and you're going to make that transaction."

"It's too late, the bank will be closed."

Erica laughed, the sound haughty. "Please, spare me your silly lies. How many times have you told me about going to the bank after hours? Security is always happy to let you in."

Jolie stood on shaky legs, a new realization sending fury pumping through her veins, giving her strength. "You knew about my mother. You used that against me. And my watch." She fingered the gold bracelet on her wrist. "Mark was as much a pawn as I was." The thought firmed her fledgling resolve.

"Not quite like you, but yes, he was a means to an end. We decided that if we had to get rid of you we might as well make a profit. We'd skim your accounts, make you look as nutty as your mother had been, then let the feds take you down. But Mark screwed up again as usual, and the feds were onto him. Brasco was furious. I had to do something to get the heat off Mark until we could get away." She smiled. "What better way to divert a man's focus than to take away something precious to him?"

All the emotion drained out of Jolie. "You killed his son." The words were just a whisper. Dear God. How could she not have seen that kind of evil in the woman she'd called her friend for so long?

"He was a pain in the ass, anyway. I have to say, I really had you going there, didn't I? Ray played you big time, did exactly what I told him to do. We had you doubting yourself all the way around. But then, no one was more surprised than he was when I killed him." Erica laughed, then shrugged indifferently. "Now that the old man's dead, too, there's no reason for me to hang around, so I'll just take the money and run. I have access to that account, too.'' She jabbed Jolie with the gun again. "Let's go."

Jolie had to do something.

She'd had enough.

SIMON DROVE AS FAST as he could across town. He had to persuade Jolie to listen to reason. Yes, he had considered her a suspect in the beginning, but that had changed. She had to believe that. He had to convince her.

His cell phone vibrated and he fished for it without letting up on his speed. He didn't like leaving Jolie's safety to anyone else. Though Brasco was dead, there was still the woman. And unfortunately, he felt certain it was Jolie's friend Erica.

"Did you get an ID?" he asked the caller, knowing from the display that it was Max.

"Three people confirmed the photo you send me of Erica Thornton with the blond hair and green eyes. She set up the account three months ago. One of the tellers remembered her because of the little mole on her cheek. She said it reminded her of some old American movie star."

Not wasting another precious second, Simon pushed the disconnect button and entered Jolie's number. He had to warn her. The agent had orders not to let anyone into her apartment, but the guy was young. And Jolie had no idea that she should fear Erica. As Simon listened to the telephone ringing on the other end of the line, he stomped on the accelerator and the engine roared, sending the car lunging forward. He might be too late already.

He skidded to a stop in front of her building and burst from the car. He jerked the door open, silently cursing the total lack of security, as he moved stealthily into the stairwell. He listened to the silence, hoping against hope he wasn't too late.

A gunshot split the air.

He lunged for the stairs, propelling himself upward as fast as he could go. Rounding the second level, he saw Erica and Jolie struggling together one flight of steps above him. Erica jerked her attention downward and took a shot at him, hitting the wall just above his head. He made an evasive maneuver, not daring to take a shot with Jolie in the line of fire.

"You bitch!" Jolie's voice. She threw herself at Erica, heedless of the weapon she wielded.

Another shot glanced off the railing. Simon had to do something. Jolie was going to get herself killed. He lunged forward as Erica pulled off another shot, grazing his arm. He grunted but didn't slow down. Another shot hissed past him.

Jolie shoved at Erica, reaching for the gun. Simon froze and took aim, his heart stalling in his chest. For a split second the weapon in Erica's hand leveled on Jolie, but Jolie was too fast for her. She rammed Erica in the midsection with her shoulder. Losing her balance, Erica grabbed at Jolie for support. Jolie twisted out of reach. And Simon took his shot, hitting Erica's wrist and sending the weapon clattering to the floor two stories below. Erica grabbed for Jolie again, but lost her balance and followed the path her weapon had taken over the railing.

Simon took the steps two at a time. Gritting his teeth against the pain, he scooped Jolie into his arms and held her close. Too weary to stand, he sank onto the closest step and held her as tightly as he dared.

"Are you hurt?" He couldn't see any visible signs

of new injury. She shook her head against his chest. "What about the agent who was guarding you?"

"I think he's dead," she said with a sob.

"I need to check on him." Simon eased her down onto the step, then leaned over the railing to make sure Erica was still lying where she'd fallen. He couldn't see how she would have survived, but he had to be sure.

He bounded up the stairs to Jolie's apartment and found the agent lying in the hall just outside the door. He was dead, all right. Simon shook his head and said a quick prayer for his family.

Sirens blared in the distance. Help was on the way, but for some it was too late. He had no sympathy for Erica. But the agent...that was a true waste. Since there was nothing he could do here, he rushed back down to where he'd left Jolie, and took her in his arms once more. She leaned against him and cried some more. He wished he could make it all go away for her, but knew it would take years to put this kind of trauma behind her.

"I'm sorry," he murmured over and over. He was sorry for the part he'd had in causing her pain. Sorry for what she'd had to go through at the hands of ruthless men like Brasco, and the betrayal by people she'd called friends.

When she drew back and looked into his eyes, he saw just how much hurt he'd wielded. That was the worst part of all. "I had a job to do," he admitted, hoping she would understand. "I had to be certain about you. But a part of me knew you were innocent right from the start."

"And when we made love?" she asked, her voice wavering.

"I knew you were innocent. I felt guilty because I couldn't tell you the whole truth." There was one other truth he couldn't tell her. That was between her and her father.

She swiped at her eyes, too weary to think clearly. "How will I ever be able to trust again? The people I thought were my friends betrayed me."

"I won't ever betray you, Jolie." Simon lifted her chin with a thumb and forefinger so that she had to look into his eyes. "Don't ever question that."

She believed him. Though her track record sucked so far, every fiber of her being believed in Simon. "What do we do now?" She winced when she noticed the blood and the tear in his shirtsleeve. She hadn't realized he'd been shot. "Besides getting you medical attention." The door below swung open and banged against the wall, announcing the arrival of the police.

"We take it slow. One step at a time." Simon kissed the tip of her nose. "I don't want to lose you, Jolie."

She smiled. How it was possible after all she'd been through, she couldn't say, but there it was. And it reached all the way to her heart.

"I'm sure there are banks in Chicago," she said, her tone teasing, but the words completely serious. She paused as two officers rushed up the stairs.

Simon gestured to the next floor with his good arm. "There's an agent down up there. Call Special Agent Johnson of the FBI and let him know. The shooter's a couple flights down."

"Yeah, we saw her. Agent Johnson is on his way. He's the one who put through the 911." The first officer surveyed Jolie, then Simon. "You two okay?"

"I'm going to need a few stitches." Simon glanced at his arm.

"Paramedics are on the way, too."

Simon assumed that Max had put in a call to Johnson when Simon reacted the way he had to the information he'd passed along. Johnson would know what that meant, the same as Simon had.

Jolie touched her throat and the bandages there. She and Simon had both been extremely lucky today.

Simon helped her to her feet and they started down the stairs. "You were saying?" he prodded.

Jolie felt almost embarrassed now that she'd said so much. Maybe he didn't want her following him to Chicago.

Simon turned her face into his chest as they passed where Erica had fallen. Jolie was thankful for that. She didn't want to see.

Once they were outside, he hesitated before going over to meet the paramedics. "Tell me what you were going to say."

She shrugged, unable to meet his gaze. "I was just thinking that a change of scenery would be nice."

A grin spread across his handsome face. "I know just the place. It's fully furnished. Even comes with a number of perks." A wicked gleam sprang to life in those sinfully dark eyes.

Jolie was the one grinning now. "Wow. I don't see how I can pass up an offer like that."

He pulled her to him again and traced the curve of her cheek with one fingertip. "You won't regret it."

"Go." She pushed him away. "You need stitches, remember?"

Reluctantly, he allowed the paramedic to do his job. Jolie kept her distance. She had to think this through. An old familiar fear had suddenly crept back into her heart. What about her mother? What if she married Simon and had children and then got sick? How could she do that to him? To their children?

The realization zapped the hope and happiness right out of her and she barely stayed vertical. Tears slipped down her cheeks. She couldn't do this. It wasn't fair to Simon.

"Jolie!"

She turned at the sound of her father's voice. He was running toward her, his face contorted with worry. How had he found out…? She didn't care. She was just glad to see him.

"My God!" He surveyed the scene around them. Another ambulance was arriving. More police cars. "What happened?"

She sagged against him. "It's a long story, Dad. I can't talk about it right now."

He hugged her to him, his strong arms comforting. "My neighbor called and said he'd heard this address go out on his police band scanner. I rushed right over. Thank God you're all right."

She shook her head, a fresh wave of tears welling. "I'm not all right." She pulled out of his arms and stared up at him, too exhausted to manage anger. But frustration twisted inside her, cutting off her breath. "I'm never going to be all right. What happened to Mother could happen to me. And I can't take that risk."

She didn't try to explain, not even to banish the look of worry and confusion on his face. He looked away from her in defeat, staring at the ground between them a moment before meeting her gaze again.

"Enough," he said wearily. "I should have told you this years ago, but I just couldn't."

Uncertainty immediately overshadowed the frustration, but did nothing to alleviate the pain breaking her heart. "What're you talking about?"

"Jolie, you can't inherit your mother's illness because she wasn't your biological mother, just as I'm not your biological father. We adopted you when you were only a few weeks old. It was all very secretive. We couldn't go through the normal channels due to our age." He shook his head wearily. "We loved you just as if you were our own."

She staggered beneath the weight of that news. "Why didn't you tell me?"

He shook his head in resignation. "I didn't want to lose what we had. I didn't want you to see me any differently. I was selfish."

She threw her arms around him and hugged him fiercely. "Don't be ridiculous." The news was unsettling, yes, but it didn't change how much she loved her father. Or how much she'd loved her mother. Now she knew why he'd never wanted to talk about her mother's illness. "I love you, Dad."

"I love you." He set her at arm's length. "Now, I don't ever want you to bring up that subject in this context again. Agreed?"

Jolie nodded, so relieved, so exhausted. Her emotions had been through the ringer. "Agreed."

Her gaze suddenly collided with Simon's. He gave her a little wave. The paramedic was still working on his arm.

"Dad, there's someone you need to meet."

"Hmm? Who is it?"

Jolie could have sworn she saw a glimmer of moisture in her father's eyes. But he blinked it away, to keep up his stoic demeanor. Always the strong one.

Jolie pointed to Simon. "You see that great looking guy over there?"

"I do indeed."

"That's the guy I plan to spend the rest of my life with."

Her father smiled down at her, pride clear in his eyes now. "Well, I certainly hope he knows what a lucky man he is."

Jolie's gaze settled on Simon's once more. "Oh, I think he knows."

"Perhaps I should ensure that he does." Her father winked. "Just in case."

Jolie watched as her father introduced himself to Simon, and she smiled. Life really was good. In spite of all the horrors she'd lived through these past few days, seeing the two men she loved together, safe and happy, made it all worth it.

Right then and there, amid the aftermath of death and betrayal, she realized for the first time in her life that the old saying her father had preached when her mother was so ill, and even after her death, was really true.

Love does conquer all.

Epilogue

Victoria reviewed the status of her active investigators as she waited for Max to join her in the conference room. She'd opted for holding this meeting there instead of in her office to allow for a more relaxed atmosphere. Whenever the Colby Agency celebrated, this was the room where they did it. Though a great deal of business was conducted in this room as well, most considered it the gathering place rather than the meeting place.

Simon and Jolie were off on their honeymoon, a cruise to an exotic location in the Caribbean. Victoria smiled. It had been ages since she'd taken a real vacation. She should do that. The image of Lucas Camp flitted through her mind. She'd come very close to losing him a few months ago. She'd been thinking about spending more time with him ever since. But something always got in the way. She'd have to make Lucas a priority. Warmth spread through her at the thought. Yes, she wanted that. For the first time she could admit to having needs—a woman's needs.

Forcing her thoughts back to the review of her staff, she noted that Ethan Delaney had requested a few months leave to be with his wife and new son.

Ian and Nicole were expecting again as well. Victoria hurried past those notations. She was immensely happy for Ethan and his lovely wife, and for Ian and Nicole, but the past had been getting in the way again lately.

She promised herself every night that she wouldn't let Leberman haunt her a moment longer. But somehow he always did. He'd find a way to slither back into her thoughts and dreams, making her relive that part of her past that she so wanted to forget. Why hadn't he died on that godforsaken island?

"Good afternoon, Victoria."

She looked up to find Max strolling into the conference room, and was grateful for his timely appearance. She would not think about the past anymore today.

"Please join me." She gestured to the chairs lining the long, polished mahogany table. "I'd like to discuss something with you."

Pierce Maxwell, aka Max, settled into a chair and gave Victoria his undivided attention. Max was a good investigator. He was quickly moving up around here. Both Ian and Simon had commended him on several occasions. That was precisely why Victoria needed him to agree to her request.

"Douglas Cooper is on the verge of being ready for his first lead assignment. His research skills have proved to be a valuable asset to the agency already. I'd like to get him into the field as soon as possible."

Max shrugged. "I don't see a problem with that. I've observed him in a number of training settings. He's competent."

Max chose his words carefully, Victoria noted. "I

agree. What I'd like is for you to take him as backup on your next assignment.''

His posture changed instantly.

Victoria knew that Max had a slight hangup where Douglas was concerned. She had come to the conclusion that Max felt Douglas hadn't quite paid his dues just yet. But Victoria knew differently. Dues were paid in many different ways. No one knew that better than she. ''Both Simon and Ian think he's ready,'' she added, when Max didn't immediately respond.

He spread his hands and shrugged slightly. ''I can do that.''

It was Victoria's wish for all of her investigators to bond, to become like family. So far Douglas was the only one she'd ever brought on board who didn't mesh with the entire team. She knew it was his background. He didn't open up easily, which made him seem unapproachable. If anyone could bring resolution to that one ripple in the fabric of continuity here, Max could.

''I'd like Douglas to fit in,'' she said candidly. ''Make that happen for me, Max. I'm counting on you.''

The blond, blue-eyed charmer stood and flashed her one of those all-American smiles. ''You got it, boss.''

Pride welled in Victoria as Max took his leave. She was indeed lucky. The Colby Agency was the best. And the men and women who made up its ranks were the reason.

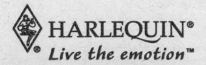

From the bestselling author
of *The Deepest Water*

KATE WILHELM

SKELETONS

Lee Donne is an appendix in a family of overachievers. Her mother has three doctorates, her father is an economics genius and her grandfather is a world-renowned Shakespearean scholar. After four years of college and three majors, Lee is nowhere closer to a degree. With little better to do, she agrees to house-sit for her grandfather.

But the quiet stay she envisioned ends abruptly when she begins to hear strange noises at night. Something is hidden in the house…and someone is determined to find it. Suddenly Lee finds herself caught in a game of cat and mouse, the reasons for which she doesn't understand. But when the FBI arrives on the doorstep, she realizes that the house may hold dark secrets that go beyond her own family. And that sometimes, long-buried skeletons rise up from the grave.

> "The mystery at the heart of this novel is well-crafted."
> —*Publishers Weekly*

*Available the first week of July 2003
wherever paperbacks are sold!*

Visit us at www.mirabooks.com

MKW749

Is your man too good to be true?

Hot, gorgeous AND romantic?
If so, he could be a Harlequin® Blaze™ series cover model!

Our grand-prize winners will receive a trip for two to New York City to
shoot the cover of a Blaze novel, and will stay at the luxurious Plaza Hotel.
Plus, they'll receive $500 U.S. spending money!
The runner-up winners will receive $200 U.S.
to spend on a romantic dinner for two.

It's easy to enter!

In 100 words or less, tell us what makes your boyfriend or spouse a true romantic
and the perfect candidate for the cover of a Blaze novel, and include in your submission
two photos of this potential cover model.

All entries must include the written submission of the contest entrant, two photographs of the model
candidate and the Official Entry Form and Publicity Release forms completed in full and signed by
both the model candidate and the contest entrant. Harlequin, along with the experts at
Elite Model Management, will select a winner.

For photo and complete Contest details, please refer to the Official Rules on the next page. All entries
will become the property of Harlequin Enterprises Ltd. and are not returnable.

**Please visit www.blazecovermodel.com to download a copy of the Official Entry Form and
Publicity Release Form or send a request to one of the addresses below.**

Please mail your entry to: **Harlequin Blaze Cover Model Search**

In U.S.A.	In Canada
P.O. Box 9069	P.O. Box 637
Buffalo, NY	Fort Erie, ON
14269-9069	L2A 5X3

No purchase necessary. Contest open to Canadian and U.S. residents who are 18 and over.
Void where prohibited. Contest closes September 30, 2003.

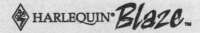

HARLEQUIN BLAZE COVER MODEL SEARCH CONTEST 3569 OFFICIAL RULES
NO PURCHASE NECESSARY TO ENTER

1. To enter, submit two (2) 4" x 6" photographs of a boyfriend or spouse (who must be 18 years of age or older) taken no later than three (3) months from the time of entry: a close-up, waist up, shirtless photograph; and a fully clothed, full-length photograph, then, tell us, in 100 words or fewer, why he would be a Harlequin Blaze cover model and how he is romantic. Your complete "entry" must include: (i) your essay, (ii) the Official Entry Form and Publicity Release Form printed below completed and signed by you (as "Entrant"), (iii) the photographs (with your hand-written name, address and phone number, and your model's name, address and phone number on the back of each photograph), and (iv) the Publicity Release Form and Photograph Representation Form printed below completed and signed by your model (as "Model"), and should be sent via first-class mail to either: Harlequin Blaze Cover Model Search Contest 3569, P.O. Box 9069, Buffalo, NY, 14269-9069, or Harlequin Blaze Cover Model Search Contest 3569, P.O. Box 637, Fort Erie, Ontario L2A 5X3. All submissions must be in English and be received no later than September 30, 2003. Limit: one entry per person, household or organization. Purchase or acceptance of a product offer does not improve your chances of winning. All entry requirements must be strictly adhered to for eligibility and to ensure fairness among entries.

2. Ten (10) Finalist submissions (photographs and essays) will be selected by a panel of judges consisting of members of the Harlequin editorial, marketing and public relations staff, as well as a representative from Elite Model Management (Toronto) Inc., based on the following criteria:

Aptness/Appropriateness of submitted photographs for a Harlequin Blaze cover—70%
Originality of Essay—20%
Sincerity of Essay—10%

In the event of a tie, duplicate finalists will be selected. The photographs submitted by finalists will be posted on the Harlequin website no later than November 15, 2003 (at www.blazecovermodel.com), and viewers may vote, in rank order, on their favorite(s) to assist the panel of judges' final determination of the Grand Prize and Runner-up winning entries based on the above judging criteria. All decisions of the judges are final.

3. All entries become the property of Harlequin Enterprises Ltd. and none will be returned. Any entry may be used for future promotional purposes. Elite Model Management (Toronto) Inc. and/or its partners, subsidiaries and affiliates operating as "Elite Model Management" will have access to all entries including all personal information, and may contact any Entrant and/or Model in its sole discretion for their own business purposes. Harlequin and Elite Model Management (Toronto) Inc. are separate entities with no legal association or partnership whatsoever having no power to bind or obligate the other or create any expressed or implied obligation or responsibility on behalf of the other, such that Harlequin shall not be responsible in any way for any acts or omissions of Elite Model Management (Toronto) Inc. or its partners, subsidiaries and affiliates in connection with the Contest or otherwise and Elite Model Management shall not be responsible in any way for any acts or omissions of Harlequin or its partners, subsidiaries and affiliates in connection with the contest or otherwise.

4. All Entrants and Models must be residents of the U.S. and Canada, be 18 years of age or older, and have no prior criminal convictions. The contest is not open to any Model that is a professional model and/or actor in any capacity at the time of the entry. Contest void wherever prohibited by law; all applicable laws and regulations apply. Any litigation within the Province of Quebec regarding the conduct or organization of a publicity contest may be submitted to the Régie des alcools, des courses et des jeux for a ruling, and any litigation regarding the awarding of a prize may be submitted to the Régie only for the purpose of helping the parties reach a settlement. Employees and immediate family members of Harlequin Enterprises Ltd., D.L. Blair, Inc., Elite Model Management (Toronto) Inc. and their parents, affiliates, subsidiaries and all other agencies, entities and persons connected with the use, marketing or conduct of this Contest are not eligible to enter. Acceptance of any prize offered constitutes permission to use Entrants' and Models' names, essay submissions, photographs or other likenesses for the purposes of advertising, trade, publication and promotion on behalf of Harlequin Enterprises Ltd., its parent, affiliates, subsidiaries, assigns and other authorized entities involved in the judging and promotion of the contest without further compensation to any Entrant or Model, unless prohibited by law.

5. Finalists will be determined no later than October 30, 2003. Prize Winners will be determined no later than January 31, 2004. Grand Prize Winners (consisting of winning Entrant and Model) will be required to sign and return Affidavit of Eligibility/Release of Liability and Model Release forms within thirty (30) days of notification. Non-compliance with this requirement and within the specified time period will result in disqualification and an alternate will be selected. Any prize notification returned as undeliverable will result in the awarding of the prize to an alternate set of winners. All travelers (or parent/legal guardian of a minor) must execute the Affidavit of Eligibility/Release of Liability prior to ticketing and must possess required travel documents (e.g. valid photo ID) where applicable. Travel dates specified by Sponsor but no later than May 30, 2004.

6. Prizes: One (1) Grand Prize—the opportunity for the Model to appear on the cover of a paperback book from the Harlequin Blaze series, and a 3 day/2 night trip for two (Entrant and Model) to New York, NY for the photo shoot of Model which includes round-trip coach air transportation from the commercial airport nearest the winning Entrant's home to New York, NY, (or, in lieu of air transportation, $100 cash payable to Entrant and Model, if the winning Entrant's home is within 250 miles of New York, NY), hotel accommodations (double occupancy) at the Plaza Hotel and $500 cash spending money payable to Entrant and Model, (approximate prize value: $8,000), and one (1) Runner-up Prize of $200 cash payable to Entrant and Model for a romantic dinner for two (approximate prize value: $200). Prizes are valued in U.S. currency. Prizes consist of only those items listed as part of the prize. No substitution of prize(s) permitted by winners. All prizes are awarded jointly to the Entrant and Model of the winning entries, and are not severable - prizes and obligations may not be assigned or transferred. Any change to the Entrant and/or Model of the winning entries will result in disqualification and an alternate will be selected. Taxes on prize are the sole responsibility of winners. Any and all expenses and/or items not specifically described as part of the prize are the sole responsibility of winners. Harlequin Enterprises Ltd. and D.L. Blair, Inc., their parents, affiliates, and subsidiaries are not responsible for errors in printing of Contest entries and/or game pieces. No responsibility is assumed for lost, stolen, late, illegible, incomplete, inaccurate, non-delivered, postage due or misdirected mail or entries. In the event of printing or other errors which may result in unintended prize values or duplication of prizes, all affected game pieces or entries shall be null and void.

7. Winners will be notified by mail. For winners' list (available after March 31, 2004), send a self-addressed, stamped envelope to: Harlequin Blaze Cover Model Search Contest 3569 Winners, P.O. Box 4200, Blair, NE 68009-4200, or refer to the Harlequin website (at www.blazecovermodel.com).

Contest sponsored by Harlequin Enterprises Ltd., P.O. Box 9042, Buffalo, NY 14269-9042.

HBCVRMODEL2

HARLEQUIN®
INTRIGUE®

presents another outstanding installment in our bestselling series

COLORADO CONFIDENTIAL

By day these agents are cowboys; by night they are specialized government operatives. Men bound by love, loyalty and the law—they've vowed to keep their missions and identities confidential...

August 2003
ROCKY MOUNTAIN MAVERICK
BY GAYLE WILSON

September 2003
SPECIAL AGENT NANNY
BY LINDA O. JOHNSTON

In **October**, look for an exciting short-story collection featuring *USA TODAY* bestselling author
JASMINE CRESSWELL

November 2003
COVERT COWBOY
BY HARPER ALLEN

December 2003
A WARRIOR'S MISSION
BY RITA HERRON

PLUS
FIND OUT HOW IT ALL BEGAN
with three tie-in books from Harlequin Historicals, starting January 2004

Available at your favorite retail outlet.

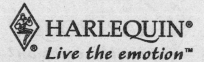

HARLEQUIN®
Live the emotion™

Visit us at www.eHarlequin.com

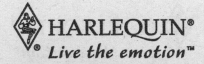